ON THE RUN

"Eric?" Elizabeth said softly. The coffee shop was deserted, and Eric was sitting at a corner table, fiddling with his pen. His jaw was set, and he was glowering.

His expression darkened when he saw her, and he immediately looked away.

"Eric, what is it? Aren't you even glad to see me?" Elizabeth cried.

Eric stared at the floor, expressionless. "Why should I be?" A muscle jerked in his jaw, and Elizabeth felt a chill run up her spine.

"Eric, we've got to talk. Alone," Elizabeth said desperately.

"Why?" Eric cried, his face contorting. "What's the use?" He searched her face, then grabbed her arm, almost roughly. "All right. You want to talk? Then let's talk." He pulled Elizabeth out of the shop and into the corridor. He was almost running and his hand hurt her arm where he gripped her so tightly.

"Liz!" Elizabeth heard her twin shriek. Jessica, spotting the two of them as they left the shop, came charging after them, her eyes filled with terror.

Elizabeth turned to look back at her twin. Something in Jessica's voice made her stop dead in her tracks.

"Forget her," Eric said gruffly. He broke into a run, pulling her after him. Soon they turned into a tiny alley around the corner and fell back against the brick wall. Eric clapped his hand over Elizabeth's mouth as Jessica ran past, and suddenly—though she knew it was crazy—Elizabeth was frightened.

Bantam Books in the Sweet Valley High Series
Ask your bookseller for the books you have missed

SWEET VALLEY HIGH
Super THRILLER

ON THE RUN

Written by
Kate William

Created by
FRANCINE PASCAL

BANTAM BOOKS
NEW YORK · TORONTO · LONDON · SYDNEY · AUCKLAND

RL 6, IL age 12 and up

ON THE RUN
A Bantam Book / June 1988

Sweet Valley High is a trademark of Francine Pascal.

Conceived by Francine Pascal.

Produced by Daniel Weiss Associates
27 West 20th Street, New York, NY 10011

Cover art by James Mathewuse

ISBN 0-553-27230-6

Published simultaneously in the United States and Canada

Bantam Books are published by Bantam Books, a division of Bantam Doubleday
Dell Publishing Group, Inc. Its trademark, consisting of the words "Bantam
Books" and the portrayal of a rooster, is Registered in U.S. Patent and Trademark
Office and in other countries. Marca Registrada. Bantam Books, 666 Fifth Avenue,
New York, New York 10103.

PRINTED IN THE UNITED STATES OF AMERICA

O   0 9 8 7 6 5 4

To Mike McGrady

One

"I hate Monday mornings," Jessica Wakefield grumbled, struggling into her jacket and flicking back her sun-streaked blond hair. She gave her twin sister a pout. "Whose idea was it anyway to work all summer? If it weren't for you, Liz, I could be in Carmel with Lila."

Elizabeth was only half-listening to her sister's complaints. Monday mornings were always busy at the newsroom where the twins were working as interns, and she wanted to glance over her notes from the previous week so she would be ready for whatever assignment she was given. "Are you ready, Jess? I promised Dan Weeks I'd be in early today."

Jessica was intent on applying her eye make-up. "Liz," she said reproachfully, "do the words *summer vacation* ring a bell? Don't you remember that it happens to be July? We're supposed to be relaxing and enjoying ourselves, not getting ulcers worrying about work."

Elizabeth giggled. Her twin's attitude toward work didn't seem to change much with the seasons. Jessica's golden rule was to make sure she had a good time—and while working as an intern at *The Sweet Valley News* might be Elizabeth's idea of fun, it didn't seem that way to Jessica. It was just one indication that the twins really were what their parents and older brother Steven liked to call them: "identical opposites."

As far as appearances went, however, even their closest friends had problems telling them apart. Both girls were five foot six inches tall and perfectly proportioned, with characteristic Southern California beauty—golden tans, shoulder-length blond hair, and eyes the blue-green of the Pacific. Each girl showed a dimple when she smiled, and the only difference between them was the tiny mole on Elizabeth's left shoulder.

But the careful observer could guess their identities by looking at their clothing. Jessica loved the latest in everything, from new hairstyles to the trendiest clothes. If something was in style, Jessica was bound to have it months before anyone else. Not even the subdued newsroom could tame Jessica's fashion sense, and that morning she had livened up her slim-cut cotton dress with a row of brand-new brooches and had tied her hair back in a bright magenta ribbon. Elizabeth preferred classic clothes. The twins' different ways of dressing was just an indication of the bigger differences between them. Jessica did things for the moment, and Elizabeth planned for the future.

Elizabeth wanted to be a writer, and she took special pains to be conscientious both in her schoolwork and in her extracurricular role as writer for *The Oracle*, the Sweet Valley High newspaper. It had been Elizabeth's idea to line up an internship at *The News* for the summer, and despite all her resistance, Jessica got roped into the project as well when her exotic schemes— such as accompanying her friend Lila Fowler to Carmel or trying to break into the movies—came to nothing. Mr. and Mrs. Wakefield believed a summer internship would be good for the twins, and they told Jessica working during the summer would teach her responsibility and help her structure her time. "I swear, Liz, having a summer job is like being in boot camp," Jessica moaned now, her eyes wide as she applied her mascara.

"You didn't mind so much when you had a crush on Seth Miller," Elizabeth reminded her. Seth was a new reporter at *The News*, just out of journalism school. With his dark curly hair and green eyes, he was very handsome.

But Jessica never stuck with anything for long, not even a crush. "Seth's OK, but he's a workaholic." Jessica sighed. Seth wrote mystery novels after hours and seemed way too busy to notice when Jessica flirted with him. Elizabeth thought Seth was avoiding Jessica for reasons other than too much work, but there was no reason to make her twin's bad mood worse that morning.

"The newsroom isn't such a bad place to be," Elizabeth pointed out. "Especially now, with all this excitement going on about the DeLucca case."

Jessica groaned. "If I have to hear one more word about the DeLucca case, I think I'll lose it." She took her lip gloss out and began to apply some color to her lips. "It's bad enough with Daddy being a lawyer. But now that Adam's living here and Steven's starting to get into it, that's all we ever hear about anymore!" She grimaced.

"It just happens to be one of the most important trials of the decade," Elizabeth said calmly. "If I were you, I'd pay a little more attention to it, Jess. In fact—"

Jessica covered her ears with her hands. "Stop it," she groaned. "Let's get going, Liz. I'd rather be at the newsroom than hear more stuff about that trial."

Elizabeth shook her head as she followed her sister downstairs and out to the carport. For the past month, Frank DeLucca had been on trial in New York for murder and racketeering, and across the country newspapers had been filled with accounts of the trial and the frustration the prosecution was experiencing in producing witnesses to testify against him. DeLucca was reported to be one of the most notorious underworld crime figures. He was allegedly responsible for countless crimes of murder, espionage, and illegal drug and gambling activities. DeLucca had been arrested several months earlier when he was caught in Brooklyn at the scene of a murder—that of a young man named Ray Underwood, who apparently had worked for DeLucca and had attempted to go clean and testify against him. So far, however, the prosecution had not produced significant evidence against DeLucca. What was so frustrating was that the police had caught a well-known criminal, but no one seemed willing to take the risk of testifying against him. All the witnesses the government had lined up suddenly became silent, and it was widely rumored that they had been paid off or intimidated by Frank DeLucca's men. The twins' father, a successful attorney in Sweet Valley, feared that DeLucca might be let off and the horrible chain of underworld crime would continue.

The DeLucca trial had gotten a great deal of attention both at *The News* office and at home. The Wakefields often talked about current events, and now that Adam Maitland was living with them for the summer, their discussions were even more lively. Adam, a classmate of Steven's at the state university, was working as an intern at a criminal law firm, Wells and Wells, during the vacation. The Wakefields had gotten very close to Adam. Earlier in the summer Laurie Forbes, his fiancée, had been the tragic victim of a murder, and Adam was accused of the crime. The Wakefields had done everything they could to help Adam, and the twins became involved—far more involved than they wanted to be—after Jessica accidentally witnessed the murderer disposing of Laurie Forbes's body.

Jessica had been through a terrible ordeal during those weeks, and Elizabeth could understand why her twin would be so unwilling to get involved in family discussions now about Frank DeLucca. "I've had it with law and crime and all that stuff," Jessica had said just the week before.

Elizabeth had decided that Jessica was just acting defensively, but she still couldn't see how Jessica could resist following the coverage of the story on TV. And Adam, who had suffered more deeply than anyone else when Laurie was killed, had taken the opposite tack. More dedicated to the law than ever, he was enraged by the trial and seemed beside himself with frustration that a criminal might be declared innocent. "Someone's got to be brave enough to testify," he had declared at dinner the night before. Elizabeth hoped he was right.

When they arrived at the office that morning, Elizabeth and Jessica walked right into a heated discussion of the trial between Seth Miller and Dan Weeks, the two youngest reporters on the paper. Dan, who had gotten quite a bit of acclaim for his coverage of Laurie Forbes's murder earlier in the summer, had become Seth's rival, and the two seemed to be arguing more and more frequently.

"If you think DeLucca's going to be convicted, you're nuts," Dan was saying to Seth. "What person in his right mind is going to testify after what happened to Underwood? DeLucca would have him killed in a second."

"I don't believe that," Seth said vehemently. "I think if someone knows something that could help convict DeLucca, he'll come forward."

Jessica rolled her eyes. "I'm going to my desk," she said to Elizabeth.

But just then Mr. Robb, the editor of *The News*, came out of his office with a girl who looked about seventeen. She had silky red hair, brown eyes, and a smattering of freckles, and was eying the twins with obvious curiosity. "Jessica and Elizabeth, I want you two to meet Darcy Kaymen," said Mr. Robb. "She's going to be joining the paper as an intern for the rest of the summer, and I'd like you both to help show her the ropes."

Darcy tossed back her hair. "We just moved here from Ohio," she said. "My father knows the man who owns this paper, so he arranged for me to come in and help out." She gave the twins a smug smile. "I love newspapers. I think this office is so *exciting*."

Elizabeth gave the new girl a welcoming smile. "I'll be happy to show you around, Darcy. Be sure to let me know if there's any way I can help."

"I'm sure I won't need much help," Darcy said haughtily. "I learn *very* quickly."

Mr. Robb returned to his office, and Seth turned up the volume on his radio, in order to listen to the morning news discussion of the DeLucca trial.

"Oh, are you listening to the trial?" Darcy asked. "My father says there's no way Frank DeLucca will go to jail. He thinks this is all just being staged by the media so it will look like the legal system in this country really works. In fact, my father thinks—"

Jessica couldn't constrain herself. "What does your father do?" she asked.

"He's a businessman," Darcy replied. "But he knows all sorts of things about law, too. And he's certain this trial is going nowhere!"

Seth looked at her mildly. "Well, quite a few people seem to think that, but I'm not one of them. I happen to think that someone will come forward to testify."

Darcy looked embarrassed and began to fidget. "Well, you could be right," she said quickly.

"I agree with Darcy," Dan cut in. "Look, Seth, no one's going to take that kind of risk. It would be suicide to testify against a man as powerful as Frank DeLucca! Face it. This trial is pointless!"

"I guess I have a higher opinion of people than you do," Seth said calmly.

Elizabeth couldn't keep quiet any longer. "I

agree with Seth," she said passionately. "I think most citizens are amazingly brave. In fact—"

Dan started to laugh. "Sounds like we have our own personal legal crusader in this newsroom," he said.

Darcy laughed with him, covering her mouth with her hand. Elizabeth felt distinctly uncomfortable. "I didn't mean to sound that way," she said, stung. "It's just that I think it's unfair to be so cynical without giving people a chance."

Darcy, sensing she had Dan's support, couldn't be stopped now. "My father says people never do anything unless they can make money out of it or get something for themselves." She gave Elizabeth a smug smile. "I guess *you* see things differently," she added.

Elizabeth felt terrible. How had things gotten off to such a bad start with the new girl? Had she done something to anger Darcy? It certainly seemed as though Darcy disliked her—even though they had barely been introduced!

Elizabeth still wanted to protest what Darcy was saying, but she felt it wouldn't do much good. The discussion was beginning to seem pointless. "Maybe I should go back to my desk and look at those page proofs," she said to Seth.

Seth leaned over and patted her on the hand. "Don't worry about being a 'crusader,' " he said affectionately. "I think you're right, Liz. There's no reason to condemn the public. If someone can testify against Frank DeLucca, I bet they will."

Elizabeth didn't feel much better, despite Seth's heartening words. She couldn't stand to think people were as fearful and self-interested as Darcy and Dan insisted. She just hoped that someone would come forward and prove them wrong!

"Come have lunch with Darcy and me," Jessica begged her twin. It was later that morning, and Jessica, who had spent one hour reading a back issue of *Vogue* and another trying out new hairstyles in the bathroom, was tired of the newsroom. She wanted to take Darcy to the coffee shop down on the first floor.

"I don't know," Elizabeth said hesitantly. "I get the impression Darcy doesn't like me very much, Jess. She hasn't been very friendly to me this morning."

In fact, that was an understatement. Elizabeth had tried to make up for their first exchange by approaching the redhead at her desk, eager to learn more about her and her background. Darcy had rebuffed her. Each time she tried to start a conversation, Darcy walked away.

Elizabeth couldn't imagine how she had offended her, but she guessed it was more sensible to avoid her for the time being than to deliberately seek her out.

Jessica pouted. "You and I never like the same people, Liz. I think Darcy seems great! Do you know she went to the same private school in Ohio that Cliff Benjamin went to?" Cliff Benjamin was Jessica's most recent discovery—a midwestern actor who had starred in a number of teenage movies.

"Well, I think I'll stay here and eat lunch at my desk," Elizabeth said. "You go ahead, Jess. Actually, it'll be good for me to stay here and get some more work done."

Jessica looked distressed. "You never like anyone *interesting*," she objected. "You always like people like Jeffrey and Enid Rollins."

Elizabeth laughed. "What's wrong with that? Enid's one of the nicest girls on earth. And you know how special Jeffrey is."

Jessica grimaced. "*Special* isn't the word I'd choose. Jeffrey's kind of tame, Liz. Besides, he's hours away at that summer camp. You can't just sit inside and work all summer. Come with us, Liz, please. Give Darcy another chance."

Elizabeth sighed. "OK," she said. "I'll go with you." Maybe she *had* been a little too hasty in assuming Darcy Kaymen didn't like her. And if they were all going to be working together, Elizabeth thought, she really ought to make an effort to get along with the new intern.

Jessica kept up a steady stream of chatter as the three girls left the newsroom together. "Let's go somewhere besides the coffee shop. Maybe the Box Tree Café," Jessica suggested. "It's her first day, right? We need to celebrate."

Darcy smiled. "That sounds like a good idea. I'm so glad you're here to show me around, Jessica." She didn't look at Elizabeth. "With your help, I should figure out how to have a good time at *The News*. I was afraid it was going to be a long boring summer. When Daddy said he thought I should get a job. . . ." She shuddered. "And newspapers! What could be more boring?"

Jessica looked delighted. "I know just what you mean," she said sympathetically. "You poor thing. I can't believe your dad made you get a job before you even had a chance to meet anyone or get to go to the beach or anything!"

Elizabeth sighed. Just what her twin needed—someone to complain to about working at *The News!* "I think it's a great job," she said loyally. "The editors are really taking a chance on us. We ought to consider ourselves lucky, to learn all we can about working on a newspaper."

Darcy looked at Elizabeth as if she were insane. "Who cares how a paper works? If Daddy didn't know the owner, I could be working at a clothing store or something fun like that. *And* getting a discount on clothes," she added significantly.

Elizabeth didn't say anything. This obviously wasn't the right topic to make her and Darcy get along better!

But Jessica looked positively enraptured. "Oh, you like clothes, too? Wait till I introduce you to my friend Lila Fowler! Her father owns a computer company, and she spends an absolute fortune on clothes! She's got the most amazing new fashions from Europe—clothes straight out of *Vogue*. I can take you to the mall, too, and show you all the best stores."

Darcy grinned. "Jessica, you're incredible! I'm so glad Daddy forced me into working at *The News*. Otherwise, I'd never have met you, and I wouldn't know the first thing about this town!"

Jessica glowed. The prospect of filling Darcy Kaymen in on everything Sweet Valley had to offer obviously appealed to her.

Elizabeth, on the other hand, was beginning to think that she and Darcy would never become friends. The redhead struck her as spoiled and shallow. And Elizabeth didn't like the way Darcy complained about being an intern at *The News*. Elizabeth felt they were all terribly lucky to be given the responsibility, and they ought to behave that way. She was a pretty good judge of character, and her sense about Darcy was that she was unlikely to be very much help around the newsroom. And Elizabeth couldn't help feeling that she wouldn't be a very good influence on her susceptible twin sister, either!

But worst of all, she knew Darcy had taken a strong dislike to her. Throughout lunch the redhead ignored Elizabeth, talking animatedly to Jessica and making Elizabeth feel like a fool for even being there. Just before they left, when Jessica was paying the check, Darcy turned to Elizabeth with a mean little flash in her eyes.

"Thanks for lunch—*Crusader,*" she said coldly.

Elizabeth bit her lip. She had clearly managed to make an enemy. Working in the newsroom was going to be very different from now on!

Two

Tuesday evening Mr. Wakefield brought take-out Mexican food home, and the whole family, along with Adam, ate dinner out on the patio overlooking the swimming pool. It was a mild summer evening, and everyone was enjoying eating outside. Mrs. Wakefield, who had changed out of her navy dress into a pair of comfortable pants, helped herself to a second taco.

"I really shouldn't," she chided herself. "But this food is so good!"

Steven laughed. "Mom, you can't weigh an ounce more than the twins do. You could pass for a model!"

"I agree with that," Adam seconded.

Mrs. Wakefield blushed. It was true that she looked young, with her sleek blond pageboy and slender figure. In her profession as an interior designer, it helped to look well put-together.

"Darcy heard about this new fad diet that makes you lose twenty pounds a month. All you do is eat grapefruit and rice," Jessica said.

"I wish Darcy would quit talking and start doing some work around the office," Elizabeth said irritably.

"That isn't very nice, Liz. It's her first week," Jessica said. "She's still getting used to things."

"Who's Darcy?" Steven asked with interest.

Steven, the twins' eighteen-year-old brother, loved mediating when the girls argued. He was pretty good at it, too. Dark-haired and handsome, Steven bore a strong resemblance to Mr. Wakefield.

"She's a new intern at the paper. Liz doesn't like her because she took Dan Weeks's side yesterday when Dan and Seth were arguing about the DeLucca trial," Jessica said, licking sauce off her fingers.

Elizabeth grimaced. "Darcy's just trying to get in good with Dan, that's all," she said. "She just repeats what she's heard her father say. I don't think she really has any opinions of her own."

Mrs. Wakefield looked surprised. "Liz," she said reprovingly, "it isn't like you to judge someone you've just met so harshly. Have you really given this new girl a chance?"

Elizabeth shrugged. "Maybe not. But Jessica's right about one thing—I didn't like what she said about that trial. I get really mad when people start claiming it's just a sham, that no one would ever be willing to testify against someone so powerful."

"Well," Mr. Wakefield said with a sigh, "it's beginning to look as if that line of argument may not be so far from the truth. After all, there hasn't been one bit of evidence solid enough to lock DeLucca away. The trial will be over in a few days, and unless a witness comes forward . . ." He leaned back in his chair. "I hate to say it, Liz, but Darcy may have a point."

Elizabeth felt her cheeks burn. "Well, maybe I'm too idealistic. But I believe someone will still testify."

Adam leaned over and patted Elizabeth on the hand. "I'm on your side," he said. "I know when I was sitting in jail thinking I might have to go to prison for Laurie's murder, I felt like all the trust I had in human nature was gone. Then—when I realized what people like you were willing to do to help me, to make sure the right man was punished . . ." His voice trailed off.

"Well, I realized that there still are people in the world willing to fight for what's right."

"Still," Mr. Wakefield said slowly, "Frank DeLucca's an unusually powerful figure, and I think the murder of Ray Underwood has left real scars on the public imagination. I'm just afraid no one who knows anything will have the guts to come forward."

Everyone was silent, and Elizabeth stared helplessly at Adam, whose expression seemed to mirror her own. Closing arguments were scheduled for Thursday, and unless someone came forward in the next forty-eight hours, Frank DeLucca would certainly go free.

"Liz!" Jessica called from her bedroom, covering the telephone receiver with her hand and sounding annoyed. "It's for you—it's Jeffrey."

Elizabeth hurried to the phone in her own room as Jessica followed, saying, "Try to keep it short. Darcy's supposed to call any minute."

Elizabeth ignored this. A long-distance phone call from her boyfriend took priority over another call from Darcy, who had already called twice that evening!

"Jeffrey," she said warmly into the phone, "I'm so glad you called. I missed you so much today."

Jessica rolled her eyes and walked out of the room, and Elizabeth giggled.

"What's so funny?" Jeffrey demanded.

"Just Jessica, giving me one of her most attractive grimaces." Elizabeth plopped down on her bed. "Tell me what's going on at camp." Jeffrey was a counselor for the summer in the San Francisco Bay area, several hours north of Sweet Valley, and his letters were filled with affectionate complaints about the boys' antics.

"Not much. We spent the whole weekend teaching the bunk how to canoe," Jeffrey said. "And the whole time I missed you like mad. I can't wait till parents' weekend so I can come back home and see you. Only three weeks away now," he added.

Elizabeth twisted the telephone cord between her fingers. "I miss you, too," she said. She proceeded to fill him in on the latest details at work, including Darcy's arrival. "Jessica's convinced she's great, but I'm not so sure," Elizabeth confided. "She's—I don't know, she seems spoiled and opportunistic to me. Not really my type."

"I think I can safely assume I'd be on your side," Jeffrey said, "and not Jessica's. Just ignore both of them and keep working hard. It sounds like you're getting really good experience at the paper, and that's all that matters."

Elizabeth smiled. "You're right. Why is it you always make such good sense?"

" 'Cause I'm such a sensible guy," Jeffrey said with a chuckle. "Promise you'll take care of yourself," he added. "You sound tense."

Elizabeth sighed. "You're right. I think I'm getting way too worked up about this DeLucca thing. From now on I'm going to try to detach myself and just concentrate on enjoying my job. And on missing you," she added.

As always, it was very hard to hang up. Talking to Jeffrey meant so much to Elizabeth, and it pained her to have to put down the phone.

Elizabeth and Jeffrey had an agreement that they would talk twice a week—so they wouldn't lose touch over the summer. Their phone calls and letters really helped make the distance seem less great. In fact, as she hung up, Elizabeth thought once again how lucky she and Jeffrey were. They were so comfortable together and knew each other so well. Jeffrey was always able to identify how she was feeling, and tonight he had really helped her resolve to change her behavior. She didn't know what she would do without him—and she knew he felt the same way.

As if on cue, Jessica came barging into the room the moment Elizabeth put down the receiver. "You done? How's Jeffrey?" she demanded, almost in the same breath.

Elizabeth smiled. "He's fine. He's been teaching his bunk how to canoe." She could feel Jessica giving her one of her famous penetrating stares.

Jessica frowned. "I can't believe you, Liz. This is your second boyfriend and your second long-distance thing, too. Don't you get sick of it? Why don't you come to the Beach Disco with Darcy and me tonight? Amy Sutton told me some really cute guys from Greenwood Academy would be there."

Elizabeth shook her head. She really felt like being by herself. In fact, she couldn't think of anything she'd rather do than curl up with a novel—or write Jeffrey a letter. Not that Jessica would understand that, since Elizabeth had just spoken to Jeffrey on the phone. Anyway, the thought of another encounter with Darcy Kaymen made Elizabeth feel uncomfortable. It was hard enough trying to get along with Darcy at work!

"Well, you know what I think about long-distance love," Jessica said, picking up Elizabeth's brush and using it. "I can't even really see the point of having a steady boyfriend. It seems kind of limiting to me. I guess when Jeffrey's around, it's one thing. But when he's *hours* away teaching a bunch of kids how to canoe . . ." She shook her head pityingly. "I just hate to see you sitting inside wasting your youth and beauty," she added dramatically.

Elizabeth laughed. She knew it would astonish her twin if she told her she actually sometimes looked forward to spending an evening completely alone. "Believe it or not, I really miss Jeffrey. Though it's probably good for us to have a little bit of time away from each other, too."

Jessica put down the brush and turned to face her twin. "Good to have time away from him? That sounds bad. Are you thinking of dumping him?"

Elizabeth groaned. "Jessica, why don't you ever listen? I just meant that sometimes it's helpful for a couple to have a little time apart. I don't have the slightest intention of 'dumping' Jeffrey."

"Oh," Jessica said, disappointed. "Well, if you change your mind about the Beach Disco, come and join us. You should, you know. Darcy's starting to think you don't like her."

How could Darcy say that? Elizabeth thought she had tried as hard as she could to be friendly to the new girl.

"Tell her she's wrong," she said quietly, fighting for control. Whatever happened, she wasn't going to be babyish about Darcy Kaymen. She would keep trying to be friendly—even though it clearly wasn't going to work!

Jessica had left for the Beach Disco with Darcy at around nine o'clock, and Elizabeth found herself unable to concentrate on anything. The book she had been reading didn't seem very exciting anymore, and finally she set it aside and went down to join her parents, Steven, and Adam, who were watching a movie on TV.

Her brother was about to fill her in on the details of the movie when a news report flashed on the screen.

"This evening marks the first real breakthrough in the ongoing trial of underworld criminal figure Frank DeLucca," the broadcaster announced. "It has been announced that a surprise witness, a doctor named William Ryan from Manhattan, will testify tomorrow against Frank DeLucca. Ryan claims to be the long-time doctor of Ray Underwood, the victim of the brutal murder reported to have been ordered by DeLucca. Sources say he has important evidence against the defendant and will testify tomorrow morning. Details will follow on the news at eleven."

"Good heavens!" Mr. Wakefield exclaimed.

"Talk about an eleventh-hour victory for the prosecution! I can't believe it."

Elizabeth's heartbeat quickened. "Does this mean DeLucca will be convicted now?"

Mr. Wakefield shook his head. "It depends on what kind of evidence this man Ryan actually has. It does mean there's a chance DeLucca will go to jail, which is more than we've been able to say yet!"

"You see, Liz," Adam chimed in, "you were right. People *are* brave. This Dr. Ryan is risking his life by testifying."

"Imagine what must be going on in the Ryans' household tonight!" Mrs. Wakefield said softly. "What a courageous man," she added.

"I don't think any of us should get our hopes up yet," Mr. Wakefield warned. "There's no telling what'll happen tomorrow during the last hours of the trial." He leaned over and patted Elizabeth on the shoulder. "But Adam's right, Liz. The main thing is that Dr. Ryan *does* have the courage to go ahead and testify—just as you predicted." He gave her a special smile. "You're right to believe in people, Liz. I hope you never lose that quality."

Elizabeth didn't answer. She wondered what it would feel like to know something about a criminal like Frank DeLucca and be put in the position of having to decide to testify—and risk

DeLucca's wrath—or stay quiet and watch him go free.

She was very glad that someone had indeed stepped forward, but she was nervous, too. She just hoped Dr. Ryan's evidence was strong enough to put Frank DeLucca behind bars, where he belonged.

Three

"Come on, you guys!" Seth Miller cried, Wednesday at lunchtime. "The news is coming on. I want to find out what happened today at the trial!"

Elizabeth hurried over to Seth's desk to watch the small TV he had in from the media room to watch the news. Elizabeth was as eager as he was to hear about Dr. Ryan's testimony. Soon a small group had gathered in front of the television: Dan Weeks, Seth, Elizabeth, Jessica, and Darcy, as well as one of the typesetters, a lanky man named Paul, and the head of the editorial department, Stan Fisher.

A hush fell over the newsroom as everyone watched the broadcaster pick up his set of notes. "This morning," he began, "marked a tremendous turning point in the controversial trial of Frank DeLucca. Last night a Manhattan-based doctor named William Ryan claimed he had important evidence that he would use to testify against DeLucca. This morning Dr. Ryan revealed that evidence."

Elizabeth nudged Jessica. "Isn't this incredible?" she whispered.

Darcy gave Elizabeth a stern look. "Shhh," she said reproachfully. "I'm trying to *hear*, Liz."

Elizabeth was annoyed, but she controlled herself. What mattered was learning what Dr. Ryan had said that morning, not Darcy's behavior.

"Dr. William Ryan is a specialist in internal medicine," the broadcaster continued. "Under heavy police protection since he contacted the police yesterday afternoon, Ryan has admitted to treating Ray Underwood, the young man murdered after attempting to turn Frank DeLucca in. According to Ryan's report, Underwood developed early-onset diabetes in his late teens and was referred to Ryan for insulin therapy. Ryan saw Underwood on a regular basis for six years—during which time he was given several important pieces of evidence linking DeLucca to an international drug ring. In shocking and lengthy testimony given under oath this morning, Dr. Ryan has produced seemingly incontrovertible evidence that Underwood was indeed murdered upon DeLucca's orders."

Elizabeth couldn't believe her ears. Then DeLucca would be found guilty and go to jail after all!

"Apparently, Underwood feared that DeLucca or his men would murder him before he was able to betray their covert operations," the newsman continued. "To protect himself, he wrote out a brief statement, signed it, and delivered it to Dr. Ryan the last time he came to him for treatment. Until this time Dr. Ryan has held that signed statement in his possession."

"Wow!" Seth exclaimed.

The broadcaster cleared his throat. "This morning Dr. Ryan read aloud from this statement, which handwriting analysts have determined was in fact written by the victim, Ray Underwood. The statement is brief and to the point. In it, Underwood claims that DeLucca and two other men—he doesn't mention their names— are in fact heads of an international drug ring. Underwood's testimony seems to be an important new piece of evidence in this trial."

"That's amazing," Elizabeth gasped.

"Dr. Ryan has provided an important new piece of evidence," the broadcaster went on. "The atmosphere in the courtroom is tense. Everyone is wondering what influence this new piece of evidence will have on the case, which is expected to go to the jury tomorrow afternoon."

Seth leaned forward to snap off the news, his face jubilant. "Hooray!" he exclaimed.

Dan Weeks leaned back in his chair, his arms folded across his chest. "I wouldn't get so carried away if I were you. Think about it, Seth. A man like Frank DeLucca is awfully powerful. It's not going to be the end of his drug ring if he gets locked up, is it? He's got hundreds of people working for him."

Seth shrugged. "That may be true. But things can only change one step at a time. The fact that DeLucca gets nailed will at least serve as an example for other criminals. It may not be the end of the drug racket, but it's bound to help."

Dan shook his head. "And what about this Dr. Ryan? How long do you give him? A week? A month? He's going to be on every single underworld 'most wanted' list across the country."

Elizabeth paled. "What *will* happen to Dr. Ryan?" she asked. "Will he get killed—just like Ray Underwood?"

Seth put his hand soothingly on hers. "The

most likely thing is that he'll enter something called the government witness protection plan. The government will help him disguise himself with a new name and a new identity—and send him somewhere far away where he'll start a new life. The mob won't be able to find him.''

Elizabeth stared at Seth. She could barely imagine what it would be like to change her name and move to a new part of the world, knowing that if people ever found out who she was, her life would be at stake. She shivered. ''This Dr. Ryan is incredibly brave.''

Darcy took an emery board out of her handbag and started to file her nails. ''I knew something like this would happen at the last minute,'' she announced. ''My father said it would.''

Elizabeth shook her head. Darcy was really impossible. ''I thought your father said DeLucca would get off scot-free,'' Elizabeth couldn't resist saying. ''Didn't he think people were too self-interested to risk their lives testifying against criminals?''

Darcy's eyes flashed. ''You don't know anything about my father,'' she retorted. Elizabeth had the feeling that it would have been better to leave well enough alone. Embarrassing Darcy in front of Seth and Dan wasn't a very smart move.

And Elizabeth could tell from the look on Darcy's face that the redhead wasn't going to let her get away with it!

"I don't think it was a very good idea saying those things about Darcy's father," Jessica said. She and Elizabeth were at the copier machine, trying to get a stack of reports photocopied for Dan before his three o'clock meeting with Stan Fisher.

Elizabeth sighed. "I know. But something about her attitude just really gets to me, Jess. It always seems like she's trying to get in good with Dan and Seth. And she must quote her father a million times a day!"

"She's perfectly nice," Jessica insisted. "But" —she lowered her voice—"I do think you ought to say you're sorry or something, Lizzie. She's been giving you dirty looks all afternoon. Why don't you just go over to her desk and say something nice to her? Tell her you like her sweater or something."

Elizabeth frowned. "I'm not afraid of Darcy Kaymen. I know you like her, Jess, but, frankly, I don't. And I don't feel any burning desire to apologize to her, either."

Jessica sighed. "OK," she said, looking apprehensively in Darcy's direction.

Elizabeth didn't wait for Jessica to say anything more. Scooping up the pile of copies she had made, she hurried back to her desk and proceeded to proofread the article Dan had given her to look over on a threatened teacher strike in a neighboring town.

To her surprise, Darcy came over to her desk with a sweet smile on her face. "Is that the article Dan wanted? Why don't you let me take it in to him," she suggested. "I've got some things to take him myself."

"Thanks," Elizabeth said, surprised. "I just have to look at the last paragraph."

"Oh, never mind that," Darcy said, snatching the paper from Elizabeth's hands. Elizabeth was just opening her mouth to protest when Dan came out of his office and Darcy sauntered over to him, her eyes fixed on Elizabeth's copy.

"Here, Dan," Darcy purred. "I've got all those things you wanted." She frowned down at Elizabeth's copy. "And here's something of Elizabeth's . . . but I think—oh, dear," she said, turning back to Elizabeth with a reproachful little smile. "You didn't mean for Dan to look at this yet, did you? Not with these errors in the final paragraph?"

"What errors?" Dan asked with interest.

"But, Darcy, I wasn't finished proofreading it yet—" Elizabeth began.

Darcy shook her head. "Haste makes waste, Liz. I thought you were the one with all the journalism experience. You ought to know that," she chided.

Dan looked amused. "Darcy's right, Liz. There *are* a few corrections that need to be made in the last paragraph." He handed her back the article, and Elizabeth felt her face turn beet red. The mistakes were glaringly obvious, and she certainly would have caught them if Darcy hadn't snatched the page from her hands.

"Look, Darcy," she said when Dan had gone back into his office, "that wasn't fair. You know I wasn't done proofreading yet. Why embarrass me in front of Dan when all you had to do was give me back the article and let me finish it?"

Darcy tossed her hair back, an arrogant expression on her pretty face. "You just have to make sure to be more careful, Liz," she said coldly. "After all, this *is* an office. And we all have to make sure we're doing our very best." With that she flounced off, leaving Elizabeth fuming.

"What's wrong with you?" Jessica asked, coming over to sit with her twin.

Elizabeth shook her head. "Just the usual. Darcy's really got it in for me, Jess. She just made me look like a real jerk in front of Dan."

"I *told* you to apologize," Jessica said. "Darcy isn't the sort of girl you want to start messing with, Liz. Why don't you go tell her you're sorry for what you said about her father at lunchtime? She's very forgiving," she added. "She can't stay mad for long."

"Forgiving!" Elizabeth cried. She shook her head. "Why should I apologize, Jess? I didn't say or do anything wrong." She frowned. "And nothing I say or do is going to make it any better."

"Well, I'm not going to get stuck in the middle," Jessica declared, standing up and walking away. She stopped and looked back at her sister. "But if I were you, I'd tell her I was sorry."

Elizabeth frowned and picked up the copy she had been working on. The newsroom wasn't half as much fun to work in now that Darcy Kaymen had arrived.

"Hey," Stan said at five o'clock, "I think we all need to celebrate the fact that this DeLucca case has cracked. Why don't we all go out for a Coke?" He patted Elizabeth on the shoulder. "The interns have been working pretty hard this week, too. Maybe it's time to show them a little appreciation. What do you say, guys?"

Dan and Seth nodded their approval, and

minutes later Darcy, Elizabeth, Jessica, and the two young reporters were walking out of the office with Stan.

"Let's go to the Press Club," Stan suggested with a smile. The Press Club was actually just the name the *News* staff had given to a small diner on the corner across from the Western Building in which the newspaper office was located. The diner served sandwiches, soft drinks, and coffee at all hours and was a favorite hangout for the paper's staff.

Elizabeth felt her spirits lift as the group seated themselves in a cozy booth. She shouldn't take Darcy's behavior so personally. After all, there were bound to be differences between interns, especially at a frenetic, high-pressure place like *The News*. Elizabeth would just have to learn to relax and not take it so hard if Darcy corrected her—or acted unpleasantly. All that really mattered was that Elizabeth had the job of her dreams.

"Let's have a toast to the interns," Dan suggested when the soft drinks had been served.

Stan and Seth nodded their approval. "To the best trio of interns a paper could have," Seth said loyally, raising his glass.

Darcy smiled demurely. "It's such a wonderful opportunity, getting to work for people like you," she gushed. Remembering what Darcy had said about wishing she could work in a clothing store, Elizabeth just shook her head.

"I'd like to learn more about how you all became interested in journalism," Dan said, looking at Darcy.

Darcy smiled prettily at him. "Oh, I've always been interested in the news. My father says—" She frowned, looking at Elizabeth. "My father says I used to play reporter when I was barely old enough to talk." She giggled. "Of course, now I'm much more serious. I'd really like to make a career out of it. Back in Ohio I was one of the editors of the school paper." She lowered her gaze when she said that, and Elizabeth wondered whether or not she was telling the truth.

"Of course," Darcy added, raising her eyes and staring straight at Elizabeth with feigned sincerity, "Liz here has a totally different experience. Isn't it true you write the gossip column for *your* paper, Liz?"

Furious, Elizabeth swallowed hard. She had to take a quick sip of soda to calm herself. Jessica must have told Darcy about the "Eyes and Ears" column, she thought. But what a shabby trick to bring it up now! Not that Elizabeth was ashamed of writing the column for

The Oracle. In fact, she enjoyed the column and had always had a lot of fun with it, her sense of justice insuring that no one got hurt and the column stayed entertaining.

But by the same token Elizabeth hadn't wanted to emphasize the gossip column to Dan or Seth. It seemed kind of juvenile now that she was working as an intern for a real newspaper. Darcy knew that, and it was clear she was enjoying Elizabeth's embarrassment.

"Gossip column?" Dan repeated blankly, looking at Elizabeth. "You don't really seem like someone who would work on a gossip column, Liz."

"It isn't exactly a gossip column," Elizabeth said. She refused to give Darcy the satisfaction of getting upset. "It's a special feature called 'Eyes and Ears.' " She went on to explain what the column was like, adding that she wrote many other features for the newspaper as well— and covered news events, too—but she felt flustered and uncomfortable. Darcy was smiling triumphantly.

"Well, there's nothing wrong with that kind of thing," Seth said supportively. "A lot of people give me flack about writing mystery novels in my spare time. They complain it isn't serious enough. I always tell them as long as I have fun with my writing, I consider myself lucky."

Elizabeth gave Seth a grateful smile, but she felt embarrassed nonetheless. She was sure Darcy hadn't done any serious work for her paper back in Ohio. And even if she had, she didn't need to make Elizabeth look bad in front of the reporters!

Jessica gave her twin a stern look. Her expression reminded Elizabeth that Jessica had warned her to apologize to Darcy to avoid just this kind of thing. But Elizabeth had less intention than ever of apologizing to Darcy Kaymen. She fervently wished Darcy had never left Ohio!

The next morning the twins were driving to work late because of Jessica's last minute uncertainty about what to wear. Jessica turned the radio on and started looking for a rock music station. The news was just coming on, and as Jessica leaned over to try another station, Elizabeth said, "Hey!" and pushed Jessica's hand away. "Don't. I want to hear the latest on the DeLucca trial."

"I'm so sick of that trial," Jessica muttered, sitting back in her seat.

"After almost twelve hours of deliberation, the jury in the Frank DeLucca trial reached a decision last night before midnight," the news reporter announced. "DeLucca has been found guilty on counts of murder and racketeering. Sentencing will take place in a few weeks. It is expected he will receive a life sentence with no parole and will face further drug-related charges."

"Did you hear that?" Elizabeth asked triumphantly. "Wow, it really makes you appreciate how touch-and-go trials can be. Two days ago it looked like he was going to go free."

Jessica didn't look impressed. "*Now* can I change the station?"

Elizabeth bit back a reproach. After all, it wasn't any of her business if Jessica didn't care about justice! But she could hardly wait to get to work to share her excitement with Seth Miller.

Four

"I'm telling you, that girl is driving me nuts," Elizabeth complained to Jessica as she backed their red Fiat Spider down the driveway. It was the following week, on a Thursday morning, and the twins were headed for work. The prospect of having to deal with Darcy took away most of the pleasure from Elizabeth's usual anticipation at the start of a workday.

The incident with Dan Weeks and Darcy had been the first in a long string. Darcy seemed to have made up her mind to torture Elizabeth, and her strategy was simple: make Elizabeth look bad in front of the staff. First Darcy pointed out that Elizabeth hadn't turned in a log report for the past week detailing how she had spent her hours at work. Then she just happened to tell Stan Fisher about it. Next, Darcy complained that whoever had used the photocopier last— and she knew it was Elizabeth—had gotten paper jammed in one of the trays. Someone—Darcy couldn't say whom—had "borrowed" the dictionary and taken it from the library. Darcy acted astonished when Dan Weeks found it on Elizabeth's desk. Elizabeth was growing exhausted and irritable. She couldn't take much more.

Jessica turned the radio on. "I think you and Darcy just got off on the wrong foot," she said calmly. "Darcy's one of the nicest girls I've met in a long time. You just make her feel insecure, that's all. If you'd try a little bit harder to make her feel relaxed, she'd be as sweet to you as she is to me."

Elizabeth groaned. "Never mind," she said. "Let's just drop the subject. Talking about Darcy makes me grouchy."

Dan Weeks was just coming out of his office when he caught sight of Darcy, sitting at her desk flipping through a magazine.

"Darcy!" he said, giving her a smile. "Can I

ask you a big favor? If you're not too busy, would you mind going downstairs to the coffee shop for me? I need a caffeine fix, and I've got my hands full right now."

Trying to hide a frown, Darcy put down her magazine. She was in the middle of a good article, in *Ingenue* magazine, her favorite, on how to win and keep a man. Getting coffee was the least appealing part of being an intern, she decided. It was so degrading. "Sure," she said, forcing a smile. "You like it black, right?"

"That's right. I hate anything in my coffee," Dan said. "Thanks, Darcy. I really appreciate it. Here's some money—get yourself something, too."

Darcy tried hard to sound pleasant as she promised to be back in a minute. *What a job*, she was thinking unhappily as she put the money in her pocket and rounded the corner, heading for the corridor out to the main part of the Western Building. Why couldn't she be doing something fun this summer instead of slaving away in this dull old newsroom?

Just then she saw Elizabeth in the library, intent on reading something. Darcy ducked her head in with a secret smile. "Hey, Liz," she said pleasantly.

Elizabeth turned around inquisitively. "Oh —hi, Darcy," she said.

"Listen, I just ran into Dan, and he asked me if one of us could get him a cup of coffee—only I can't do it because Stan just told me he needs me in his office right away." Darcy handed Elizabeth a crumpled dollar bill. "Would you mind running down to the coffee shop?"

Elizabeth *did* mind, but she knew that when Stan wanted to see one of the interns, that person had to drop everything else. Besides, Elizabeth thought, Jessica might be right. Maybe she *should* make an attempt to be nicer to Darcy. Maybe she could kill her with kindness! She smiled to herself at the thought.

"How does Dan take his coffee?" Elizabeth asked.

"Cream and sugar," Darcy said. "I'd better run—thanks." She darted off, fighting to suppress an attack of giggles. She just wished she could be there when Elizabeth presented poor Dan with his cup of coffee.

The coffee shop for the Western Building was on the first floor. It was a small, brightly lit, cheerful shop, but it tended to get crowded. That morning it took Elizabeth almost ten minutes to get to the front of the long line of Western Building employees who wanted coffee or a midmorning snack. While she waited in line, she watched the boy behind the counter. From the unfamiliar way he worked the cash register and served orders, she guessed he must be new.

Elizabeth's glance kept coming back to the boy. He was unusually handsome and very appealing. He was tall—six feet, she guessed—with thick, dark hair, hazel eyes, and a strong jaw. He smiled at the customer in front of her, and she noticed he had a dimple in his right cheek. Elizabeth laughed inwardly at herself. It wasn't like her to pay so much attention to a boy—especially someone she didn't know. And she had been concentrating so hard on him that when it was her turn to order, she felt herself blush.

"Hi," he said, smiling directly at her. "Can I help you?"

Elizabeth couldn't resist making conversation before ordering. "You're new here, aren't you? I've never seen you here before."

There was no one behind Elizabeth, and the boy seemed glad to take a break. "Yes. I just started," he told her. He smiled at her, and his dimple showed again.

"Boy, it must be tough the first week on a job like this one," Elizabeth commiserated. "Especially when the whole building pours in here at the same time demanding coffee!"

"Oh, I don't mind," he said. "Actually, I kind of like it when it's busy." He looked bashful now that they were actually conversing, which made Elizabeth feel bolder.

"My name is Elizabeth Wakefield," she said, smiling at him. "But most people call me Liz. I'm working as an intern upstairs at *The News* for the summer. I'm in here all the time getting coffee for the reporters, so I'll probably see a lot of you."

"Nice to meet you, Liz," he said. He put his hand out to shake across the counter. "My name is Eric. Eric Hankman. I just moved here with my dad from Ohio, so I don't know very many people around here. It's nice to meet a customer who has time to talk! Most of the people who've been in here today are too busy to do much more than order."

Elizabeth smiled. "Welcome to Sweet Valley, Eric."

A long pause followed, and Eric looked at her bashfully—as if he wanted to keep talking but wasn't sure what to say.

"Well," Elizabeth said reluctantly, "I suppose I should get some coffee."

"One coffee, coming right up," Eric said ceremoniously. "How would you like it?"

"Cream and sugar," Elizabeth said. She watched Eric pour the coffee, wishing she could think of a reason to hang around and keep talking.

"So," Eric said, still looking shy, "do you go to school around here?"

Elizabeth nodded. "I go to Sweet Valley High. What about you? Where will you go in the fall?"

"Sweet Valley High," Eric said, looking delighted—and then embarrassed by his big smile. "I'm going to be a senior. Maybe you could . . . I don't know, show me around sometime. My dad and I don't know very much about California or anything." He reddened, and Elizabeth felt her heart go out to him. "If you wouldn't mind, that is," he added hastily.

"Eric, I would *love* to show you around Sweet Valley," Elizabeth said warmly. She handed him Dan's dollar bill and watched with sympathy as he fumbled with the cash register. "Why don't we get together one day after work? I can meet you down here, or you can come up to *The News* office."

Eric looked very happy. "That sounds great," he said, handing her change and a small paper bag with the cup of coffee inside.

Elizabeth was still smiling when she left the

coffee shop. *What a nice guy*, she thought. She smiled every time she thought about the confused expression on his face when he stared at the cash register. It would be really fun showing Eric around Sweet Valley!

The elevators were crowded, and it took almost five minutes to get back upstairs to the *News* office. But finally Elizabeth had made her way to Dan's office and tapped gently on the door.

"Dan? I brought you your coffee," she said, handing him the bag.

Dan had computer forms all over his desk and looked worried and harassed. "Oh—Liz, thanks," he said, taking the bag from her. "I thought Darcy was going to get this, but I guess she got sidetracked." He opened the bag and took the cup out, then snapped off the lid. A frown crossed his face as he stared down at the coffee.

"Is anything wrong?" Elizabeth asked.

"Well, as matter of fact, there is. I'm allergic to cream. I can only drink coffee black," Dan said. Looking exasperated, he set the cup down on his desk. "Never mind, Liz. I'll go down and get it myself."

Elizabeth was just about to explain that Darcy had *specifically* told her "Cream, sugar" when she realized what must have happened: Darcy had deliberately tried to make her look foolish again. And once again, she had succeeded.

But Elizabeth wasn't going to stoop to her level and tattle to Dan. "I'm terribly sorry. I must've misunderstood Darcy," she said calmly. "Let me go back downstairs, Dan. There's no reason for you to go." She hurried to the door. "I really want to," she added when she saw he was about to protest.

"OK, OK," Dan said, smiling as he turned back to his printout.

Elizabeth was fuming as she hurried back out to the main corridor. That Darcy Kaymen had a lot of nerve! And if it wouldn't have made Elizabeth look babyish and unprofessional, she would have told Dan Weeks exactly why his coffee order had come out so totally wrong!

"Hey!" Eric exclaimed. "You weren't kidding when you promised you'd be in here all the time! Those reporters must really be cranking to need so much coffee."

Elizabeth smiled ruefully. "To tell you the truth, I think I've gotten on the bad side of one of the other interns. She purposely told me that this reporter wanted cream and sugar in his coffee, when in fact he wants it black." She sighed. "It's a long story—and a pretty silly one, too."

Eric looked sympathetic. "That's all you need —to have one of the other interns trying to make you look bad." Her predicament seemed to put him more at ease. "I ran into a problem like that back at my old school. I was the editor of the literary magazine, and one of the staff writers really had it in for me. It turned into open warfare by the end of last school year."

Elizabeth looked at him with interest. "Are you a writer?" she asked.

Looking shy again, Eric nodded. "I write poetry," he said. "Not a very macho occupation, you've got to admit."

Elizabeth made an impatient gesture. "Who cares about macho? I write, too," she added, smiling at him. "I haven't written very much poetry, but I *have* written a few stories. I'd love to read some of your work," she added.

Eric smiled. "Well, I've got my first poem coming out in a journal next fall. But until then you'll have to put up with my lousy handwriting if you want to read anything I've written. I don't even know how to type!"

Elizabeth had forgotten all about Dan's coffee. She couldn't believe Eric Hankman was a published poet—or soon to be, at any rate! Within minutes they were talking like old friends about creative writing. Elizabeth told Eric all about her work on *The Oracle* and her efforts to line up the summer internship. Eric looked at her with admiration.

"I wish I could have a job like that. It sure beats pouring coffee," he said.

"True," Elizabeth said with a smile, "but we're not getting paid. We're working just for the experience, which means it's hard to buy typewriter ribbons!"

Eric laughed. "You're so easy to talk to," he said, smiling at her. "It's been a long time since I've felt so relaxed."

The minute he said that, a shadow crossed his face.

"Is something wrong?" Elizabeth asked.

Eric seemed to tense up. "No," he said. His voice sounded different, almost harsh. For just a split second Elizabeth thought there was something frightening about his expression.

Then he snapped out of it. "You'd better not forget this," he said gently, handing her a fresh cup of coffee. "This time it's on me. Save your money for those typewriter ribbons."

Elizabeth thanked him warmly. *He really is nice*, she thought as she hurried once more toward the elevator banks. And on top of it all, a poet!

Meeting Eric more than made up for having to go back twice for Dan's coffee. And it made Elizabeth smile to think what a favor Darcy had done her!

Five

"You guys!" Darcy exclaimed, hurrying over to the corner of the library where the twins were putting together an index of phone numbers. It was Friday morning, and Darcy had been downstairs doing a coffee run. Her cheeks were flushed with excitement, and her brown eyes were glowing. "You guys, you should see—" She was out of breath. "There's a new guy working down in the coffee shop. Have you seen him yet? He's absolutely *adorable*." She hugged herself with excitement. "Not really handsome," she hastened to add, "but there's something so cute about him—so interesting." Her eyes looked dreamy. "His name's Eric

Hankman, and you're never going to believe what a coincidence this is. He's from Ohio, just like me!"

Jessica looked up from her work with interest. "I haven't seen him," she admitted. "Liz, have you?"

Elizabeth pretended to be absorbed in the telephone book in front of her. "Yes," she said calmly. "I met him yesterday when I was getting coffee for Dan." She looked pointedly at Darcy. "I got the order wrong somehow, so I had to go back twice."

Darcy brushed this comment aside. "Isn't he fabulous?" she gushed. She threw herself down in the chair next to Jessica. "He's from Shaker Heights, a suburb of Cleveland. I'm from Toledo, so we don't actually know any of the same people. But one of my best friends moved to Cleveland last year, and I'm going to call her the second I get home to find out if she knows Eric." She shivered with excitement. "I want to find out every single little thing about him I can. You guys, you have to forgive me for complaining about working at *The News* this summer. Now that I've met Eric, I couldn't care *less* how boring it is up here." She giggled. "And from now on, all coffee orders come straight to me. I want to be sure to spend as much time down in that coffee shop as possible!"

Elizabeth frowned as she wrote down a phone number. She couldn't believe the way Darcy was carrying on. Was it possible Eric liked her? From the few moments she had spent talking to him, she couldn't imagine it. Not someone as sensitive and sweet as he seemed. How could a *poet* be interested in someone like Darcy?

But Darcy was clearly smitten. "You wouldn't believe how much information I managed to get out of him already," she boasted. "Go on, you guys. Ask me anything you want to about Eric Hankman."

Jessica was much more willing than Elizabeth to play this game. "How old is he?" she asked promptly.

"Seventeen," Darcy said at once. "His birthday's in May. He's a Taurus," she added significantly. "Stubborn, forthright, down-to-earth. And very loyal once he's made up his mind about someone," she added meaningfully.

Elizabeth slammed the phone book shut. It was impossible to work with Darcy prattling on like this. And why was it that she felt the slightest bit annoyed—even upset—that Darcy had managed to find out when Eric's birthday was?

"Go on," Darcy said triumphantly. "Ask me something else."

"Well—what's he *like*?" Jessica demanded. "He can't have very much money if he's working in the coffee shop," she added. "Does he have a car? Does he play a sport? Is he a good dancer?"

Darcy looked taken aback. Obviously she hadn't gotten around to these fine points in her interrogation. But Darcy wasn't willing to admit it. "Oh, I'm sure he doesn't care about money," she said quickly, looking disdainful. "He's far too sensitive for that sort of thing, Jess. He's a poet," she added, the dreamy look coming back into her eyes. "I can just imagine what it'll be like when he writes poems about *me*."

Elizabeth put the cap on her pen. "Excuse me," she said, getting up. "I'm going back to my desk to try to get this list done. Jess, we promised Seth we'd have it ready for him soon."

"Don't go yet!" Darcy begged. "I'm just getting started."

Elizabeth frowned. She didn't like this one little bit. She knew it was ridiculous to be disappointed that Eric had told Darcy he wrote poetry, too. After all, Darcy had probably barraged him with questions, and what was he supposed to do? He was a friendly boy, and there was no reason for him to conceal information.

All the same, she felt funny about it. She didn't like to think about Eric confiding in Darcy.

"But the thing is, he isn't one-dimensional or pretentious or anything," Darcy was going on. "He likes lots of things: bike-riding, music—he plays the guitar and has even written some lyrics—long walks . . ." She looked from one twin to the other. "He's a dream come true," she added triumphantly. "I'm not even going to try to hide the fact that I'm madly in love with him. So don't either of you try to steal him away," she admonished in conclusion.

Elizabeth couldn't believe her ears. "You're in love already?" she couldn't resist asking. "After just one conversation?"

"Not everyone has to spend months with one guy to fall in love, Liz," Jessica retorted. "Liz thinks she's the expert just because she and Jeffrey have stuck it out through thick and thin," she added to Darcy.

Elizabeth was furious. She didn't want to talk about Jeffrey just then—especially in front of Darcy. "Look, I'm going back to my desk," she snapped. She didn't know why she was feeling so defensive and out of sorts, but she felt as though she had to get away from Darcy before she started another argument.

Jessica bounced up, too. "I'm going downstairs to check this guy out," she declared. "If he's as great as you say he is, Darcy, you may have to put up with a little Wakefield competition!"

Elizabeth hurried back to her desk. Ever since

Darcy Kaymen had arrived, things around the office had gotten worse and worse.

To her dismay, Darcy followed her. "I just can't concentrate on anything," she said happily, sitting down at the chair next to Elizabeth's desk. "Liz, you've been in love before. Did you feel like this when you first met Jeffrey?"

The last thing Elizabeth wanted right then was to confide her most personal memories to Darcy Kaymen. "It's different for every person," she said vaguely, opening her manila folder and trying to look as absorbed as possible in her work.

"I'm going to go downstairs," Darcy declared. "I feel like a cup of tea or something. Can I get you anything, Liz?"

Elizabeth shook her head. "No, thanks," she said dryly.

Elizabeth had barely settled down to work when Jessica reemerged, full of the exciting news that she had met Eric Hankman. "He thought I was you," she reported. "Liz, he was *awfully* friendly. Does he have a crush on you or something? He looked heartbroken when I told him I was your twin sister and not you."

Elizabeth was suddenly sick of the subject of Eric Hankman. "I barely spoke to him," she said coolly. "Jessica, I really do want to get this project done."

"OK, OK!" Jessica cried. "Anyway," she added, "he's cute, but he isn't really my type. He looks too serious and intellectual." She grinned. "But you should see Darcy. Wild horses couldn't drag her away from that coffee counter."

Elizabeth didn't answer. She was wondering if Eric Hankman was as intrigued by Darcy as Darcy was by him.

By five-thirty that evening Elizabeth felt out of sorts. She was far behind on the research project for Seth and Dan, and in fact she felt that the whole week had been much less productive than she would have liked. Besides, she had made a fool out of herself more than once, with Darcy's help. She was going to have to work a lot harder the following week to feel that her esteem around *The News* was as high as it had been before Darcy's arrival.

To make amends, she stayed behind when Darcy and Jessica left and was still at work when the reporters got ready to go.

"Burning the midnight oil?" Seth teased her. "Come on, Liz. It's Friday night. Don't you want to go home and get ready to go out on the town with your twin sister?"

Elizabeth shook her head. "Nah. I'm in kind

of a quiet mood," she told him. "I actually feel like working."

"Well, don't stay too late," Seth warned her with a smile. "Six o'clock at the very latest, you hear me?"

Elizabeth promised him, and by six o'clock she was hungry and tired enough to put aside the project and head downstairs. Jessica had driven the Fiat home at five, and Elizabeth had to walk past the coffee shop to get out the main entrance to the street where the bus stopped. When she passed the coffee shop, she glanced in quickly to see if Eric was still there, but the shop was empty.

"Hey," a familiar voice greeted her when she stepped outside into the cool evening air. "I was hoping I'd catch you!" It was Eric. He was leaning up against the building, looking every bit as nice as she remembered, and smiling directly at her. "I know for a fact that your sister took the car home because she and Darcy stopped in to say goodbye," he added. "So how about letting me give you a lift home?"

Elizabeth was really happy to see him. "Thanks," she said, feeling strangely shy. "As long as it isn't too far out of your way. Where do you live, anyway?"

Eric mentioned the name of the street, but

Elizabeth didn't recognize it. He assured her it was no problem to give her a ride.

"My dad and I don't eat till late on weekend nights. He works late," Eric said.

"Really? What sort of work does he do?"

"Oh—he's a businessman," Eric told her. "Come on. My old wreck of a Dodge is in the garage."

Elizabeth smiled when she saw the car. It was very big, for one thing, and looked at least ten years old. "Did you drive this out from Ohio?"

Eric's eyes clouded over. "Nah. I had to sell my car. We got this used."

"Do you miss Ohio?" Elizabeth asked, getting into the passenger's seat.

Eric shrugged. "No, not really." He didn't seem particularly eager to talk about Ohio, and Elizabeth wondered how Darcy had pumped so much information from him.

"Darcy's from Ohio, too, right?" she continued.

Eric turned the key in the ignition. "Yeah," he said. "That's what she said. Listen, Liz, about that tour of Sweet Valley we talked about yesterday—are you still willing?" He smiled at her, and she thought again how nice he looked when his dimple showed.

"Of course. Whenever you say," Elizabeth assured him.

"How about tomorrow afternoon? I'll treat you to dinner afterward—if you don't mind driving around in this old boat," Eric said shyly.

Elizabeth laughed. "No. That sounds like fun. But will you do me a favor?"

Eric looked alarmed, and Elizabeth wondered why he suddenly seemed so ill-at-ease. "What favor?" he asked, backing the car out of the garage.

"Will you bring some of your poetry tomorrow? And I'll bring some things I've written, too," Elizabeth said.

He smiled, a look of relief crossing his face. "That sounds good." They drove for a little while in companionable silence. "You know, I feel really lucky to have met you," he said after a few moments. "You know what it's like— moving and everything. You feel as if your whole life is disrupted and nothing will ever be the same again."

"Why did you move? Was your father transferred?" Elizabeth asked.

A shadow crossed Eric's face. "Yes," he said abruptly.

"Will you be able to visit your old friends in Ohio? Or maybe they can come out here," Elizabeth said.

Eric shook his head. "It isn't that way, though. Once you move, you move. But I don't really want to think about that," he said firmly. "I'm here now, that's what matters." He smiled, though with an effort. "And I'm glad I met you, Liz."

Elizabeth smiled back at him. "I'm glad I met you, too," she said.

And she meant it. She was really looking forward to spending the next day with him. She just hoped Darcy didn't find out about it!

Elizabeth didn't really think about whether or not to tell Jessica about her plans with Eric until Jeffrey called later that evening. Jessica was over at Darcy's house, and Elizabeth had just taken a bath and was about to start a book she'd been looking forward to reading when the phone rang.

"Liz? It's me. Jeffrey," he said, his voice sounding husky.

"Jeffrey!" Elizabeth was delighted. She hadn't expected him to call that evening.

"I've been missing you so much I just had to call you," Jeffrey said. His voice sounded sad and lonesome.

"Oh, Jeffrey, I miss you too," Elizabeth said.

"You seem so far away," he continued mournfully. He paused. "I was afraid you might be out," he added. "I mean, it's Friday night and everything."

Elizabeth laughed. "Where would I be, exactly?" she teased him.

"I know you're going to think this is ridiculous, but I've been getting the most horrible pangs of jealousy," Jeffrey said. "Every time I think about you and start imagining all the guys who must think you're as beautiful as I think you are . . . it's just starting to get to me, being so far away from you," he concluded.

Elizabeth was surprised by how sad he sounded. It wasn't like Jeffrey to be jealous—especially without a reason. Thinking about Eric, she felt a sudden twinge.

"You know you don't have anything to worry about, you silly thing," she admonished. "Look, here it is Friday night, and you know what I've been doing? Taking a bath and getting ready to read a book." She giggled. "Not exactly a lurid evening."

Jeffrey cleared his throat. His voice sounded emotional. "I know it's dumb. I tried not to call you tonight because I was afraid of sounding like a jerk. But I just wanted you to know how much I love you—and how much I miss you."

Elizabeth felt a wave of intense affection for him then. "I miss you, too," she said softly. "I wish we could be together tonight instead of just talking on the phone."

"Well . . ." Jeffrey sounded as if he hated to

hang up. "Take care of yourself, and I'll call next week. OK?"

"OK," Elizabeth said softly. Replacing the receiver, she felt strangely sad, and she decided then not to tell Jessica—or anyone—about her plans with Eric. Not that she had any reason to feel guilty about it. After all, Eric was a new friend, and she was doing the most natural thing in the world, showing him around Sweet Valley.

Still, she couldn't see the point of telling Jessica about it. If she and Eric were going to become friends, no one had to know about it but the two of them. Certainly not Jessica—or even Jeffrey.

Six

"OK," Elizabeth said, turning to Eric with a smile. "Where to first?"

"You're the tour guide," Eric said, sitting back in the passenger seat of the Fiat. "You tell me. What should I see?"

Elizabeth thought it over. "Well, it depends. Do you want the one-hour tour or the deluxe, all-afternoon tour?"

"Oh," Eric said quickly, "definitely the deluxe. I want to see every last corner of this town!"

Elizabeth laughed and started the Fiat up. She had decided that if she was giving Eric a tour, it would be easier if she drove, rather than constantly giving him directions. That turned out to have been a good idea because Jessica had invited Darcy over to the Wakefields'. The two girls had been more than a little curious about where Elizabeth was going—and where she was taking the Fiat. Elizabeth had invented a white lie about taking Enid Rollins to the beach.

"Let's start with the big picture," she said. "I'll take you up to Miller's Point to see the whole valley. How does that sound?"

Eric smiled. "I'm in your hands," he said.

Elizabeth turned the red Fiat convertible up a steep hill. She couldn't help noticing how nice Eric looked. His dark, thick hair was neatly combed, and he was wearing a pair of faded jeans and a white cotton shirt that showed off his tan. There was something so intriguing about his face, too—a slightly mysterious quality that made her want to look at him again and again.

"This is Miller's Point," Elizabeth told him, stopping the car at the highest point on the bluff overlooking the valley. "A notorious parking spot," she added with a smile, "but it also happens to have the most spectacular view around. Let's get out of the car so I can show you the view." She turned off the engine, and they got out of the Fiat to inspect the breathtaking view of the valley, the town, and the Pacific, sparkling blue-green in the distance.

"God, it's so beautiful," Eric murmured, staring out at the ocean. He turned back toward her and smiled. "It reminds me of your eyes, do you know that?"

To her embarrassment, Elizabeth felt her cheeks turn red. "Look," she said quickly, pointing. "You can see the mountains starting there. I love this spot," she added quietly. "It's so high up here—so far away from everything."

Still staring at the sea, Eric nodded. "I know what you mean." He put his hands in his pockets. "I'd love to take a boat sometime and sail all the way across," he said softly. "Imagine what it would feel like days and days from anyone, with only the water around you."

Elizabeth shivered. There was something haunting in his voice. "Wouldn't you get lonely?" she asked him. "I think I'd rather have some friends around."

Eric shook his head. A shadow crossed his face, and Elizabeth thought his eyes looked fierce. "Who needs people?" he demanded. "I think it would be much better alone—just me and the sea."

Elizabeth suddenly felt nervous. A muscle twitched in Eric's cheek, and she remembered the moment in the coffee shop when his mood had suddenly darkened. Had she made him angry somehow? Something seemed to be troubling him. "Well," she said at last, "maybe we should drive into town."

Eric seemed to snap out of his mood. "OK," he said, smiling at her. But the strange expression was still there in his eyes. It seemed as if he were straining to be at ease again, to recapture his former lighthearted air. But it was only half-working.

"Tell me more about you," he said when he got back in the car. "So far all I know is that you're sixteen, you like to write, and you have a twin sister named Jessica, who I keep confusing with you." His voice sounded a little more natural, and Elizabeth relaxed slightly.

"Here's an easy way to tell us apart—look at the wrists. Jessica never wears a watch. She goes by what my brother Steve calls 'Jessica Standard Time'—which means she's late about ninety-nine percent of the time."

Eric smiled. "What about you? I bet you're never late."

Elizabeth started the engine again. "Not usually. That's one of the problems of being an 'identical opposite,' though. Another family term," she explained when Eric looked confused. "Jessica and I are so different that people tend to expect she's going to act one way and

I'm going to act another. Sometimes we're not as totally opposite as everyone expects."

"Which means I can't always count on you to be on time?" Eric teased.

Elizabeth shook her head, her blond ponytail bobbing. "Not that. It's just that I sometimes feel that I can't be as earnest and responsible as my family—Jessica especially—expects."

"I know what you mean," Eric said thoughtfully.

Elizabeth turned the Fiat toward the high school. "I've talked a lot about my family," she said. "What about yours? You haven't told me a thing about them."

Eric shrugged. "There isn't much to tell. There's just me and my dad," he said rather abruptly. Elizabeth waited for him to explain, but he didn't say anything else. He seemed to be concentrating on the car in front of them as they reached the road in front of the school. His jaw was clenched, and he tapped his fingers nervously on the dashboard.

Elizabeth glanced sideways at him. What was it about Eric? What was he trying to hide? she wondered to herself. But aloud she said only, "Here's Sweet Valley High. But I'm sure you've already seen it." She was always surprised by how quiet and serene the building and grounds looked with no students around.

Eric nodded. "It's a nice school. I bet I'll like it."

Elizabeth watched him for a moment. She was so curious about Eric! She wondered what had happened to his mother, but she was afraid to pry. Eric certainly didn't seem to invite questions.

In fact, by the end of the afternoon Elizabeth had become aware of a pattern in Eric's behavior. As long as the conversation centered on Elizabeth—her family, her hobbies, her friends—Eric was open, friendly, cheerful, full of questions and remarks. But the minute Elizabeth tried to turn the conversation back to him, he closed up. She could see his expression change the second she asked him anything about himself. That dark, almost angry shadow crossed his face, and he tensed up. It made her almost afraid of him. Then the moment would pass, and he would be himself again—sweet, open, friendly.

Elizabeth didn't know what to make of him. Was he just shy, or was he trying to hide something from her? Or had he suffered some kind of trauma that he wasn't yet ready to reveal?

"Look," she said after they had driven through the town, looked at the beaches, passed the favorite local restaurants, and ended up at Secca

Lake, a small, pretty lake in a park several miles outside town, "this is where the deluxe tour ends. What do you say we get out here and take a walk? Or maybe sit under those trees and read each other's writing for a while?"

"The second idea sounds good. I'd really like to read your stories," Eric said."

Elizabeth parked the car, and they gathered their notebooks up, then headed for the quiet privacy of a grove of trees near the lake. For some time they read in silence. Elizabeth had chosen a story for Eric to read called "Futures," about a young girl working as a companion to two elderly women. In the story, the young girl, Allison, learned a great deal about courage and trust from the way the two elderly sisters treated each other. It was a new story, and one of her best, Elizabeth thought.

Eric gave her two poems to read. The first, called "Harvest," was one of the most mournful poems she had ever read. It was a short, lyrical description of a barren field in the Midwest. It ended so sadly Elizabeth thought she might cry.

No sparrows light here,
the sheaves picked clean,
and summer gone
with nothing left to stave off cold
or hunger.

"This is beautiful!" she exclaimed, finishing the poem. "But, Eric, it's so sad."

Eric nodded. "Yeah," he said. "That's a pretty lonesome poem."

Elizabeth turned to the second, called "Leaving You," and her eyes filled with tears. It was about saying goodbye, and the pain the speaker felt at leaving home. One stanza of the poem was about a girl, but Elizabeth feared it would be intrusive to ask about her:

> Maybe to love
> is always to hurt deeply and not just
> to hurt, but to destroy,
> knowing this
> awful farewell
> has been in store for us.

"Wow," she said, putting down the poem. "Eric, you're really talented."

"Thanks," Eric said simply. She liked the fact that he didn't try to be falsely modest about his ability. But he put his hand up to quiet her. "I want to finish your story," he told her. "Then we can talk."

Elizabeth waited patiently for him to finish. She felt unusually nervous. It was the first time she had ever shown her writing to someone her

73

own age whose work she admired so much. She began to worry, as he read, that her story was too slight, too immature.

"Wow," Eric said at last, putting the story down with a smile, "you write very well, Liz. That's a really powerful story."

They sat quietly for a few minutes, looking at the lake.

"Can I ask you something?" Eric ventured. "Do you really believe people are like that—the way you presented them in the story? You really think that old woman would risk her life, trying to save her sister?"

Elizabeth nodded. "Why, don't you think so?"

Eric shook his head. "I guess I don't. Don't get me wrong, Liz. I think your story is beautifully written, and I think you've done a really good job making these characters come to life. It's just that I don't really think people are so selfless. I guess I see the world—" He sighed. "I guess I imagine that deep down people just want to save themselves. I don't think they really try to help each other that much."

Elizabeth couldn't believe how disillusioned Eric sounded. "I don't think that's true at all," she said. "Look at a community like Sweet Valley! I can't even list the number of times I've seen this place pull together to help people who needed it." She told him about the carnival she had helped plan to raise money for special needs children, and the help she got from everyone she spoke to. "And that's just one example. This is a really special, caring place, Eric. Maybe the town where you lived in Ohio wasn't that way, but—"

"I don't think any place is that way," Eric interrupted. He had that fierce look in his eyes again, and Elizabeth felt goose bumps rise on her arms.

"Eric," she cried softly, "you sound so angry!"

His face softened. "Oh, Liz, I'm sorry. I shouldn't sound so bitter in front of you. You are the sweetest girl I've ever met." He put his hand on hers. "I don't mean to try to argue you out of your way of seeing the world. I think you're very lucky to believe in people the way you do."

Elizabeth stared at him. "Don't you trust anyone?" she murmured. "Don't you even trust me?"

Eric sighed and looked out at the lake. "My mom and dad separated several months ago," he told her. "Since then, it's just been me and my dad. We've been through a lot together, and it hasn't been an easy time. I don't really like talking about it. I guess that has something to do with why I'm edgy around people. Sometimes I just expect the worst."

Elizabeth took his hand and pressed it gently. "I hope I can make you trust me," she murmured. "I hope I can make you see that there's a lot of good in people here, too. Whatever has happened to you in the past, it won't happen here, Eric. I promise."

Eric smiled, but he still had that frightening look in his eyes.

What a strange, strange boy, she thought. He wrote such beautiful poetry, and yet his very sensitivity seemed to make him hurt every time he looked at the world!

Elizabeth hoped she could help change his mind, that she could make him see there was more good in people than evil. But she didn't think it would be a very easy task.

"I wish Elizabeth hadn't taken the Fiat. I want to go shopping," Jessica grumbled. "Darcy, can't you borrow a car from your parents?"

Darcy, flicking through one of Jessica's old yearbooks, shook her head. "Nope. I told you—my parents are both out doing errands. Hey, who's this guy? He's cute."

Darcy and Jessica had spent most of the afternoon looking through the Sweet Valley High yearbook. Although Darcy would be attending a private school, Whitehead Academy, in a neighboring town that fall, Jessica was filling Darcy in on her own friends in Sweet Valley, telling her which guys were good-looking, which girls were nice, and which students were to be avoided at all costs.

"That's Aaron Dallas. He *is* cute. He plays soccer—he's a big jock—but he has a girlfriend. Anyway, I thought Eric Hankman was the only guy for you."

Darcy shrugged. "Eric's cute. I like flirting with him, and I wouldn't mind getting to know him better. But he's a little odd, I think. Besides, why limit yourself when you're new in town? I heard Seth telling Dan that some new college intern is coming to the paper next week— Andy Sullivan. He's a sophomore at Stanford and he's going to be helping Dan out. I wouldn't mind going out with a Stanford student," she added, her eyes shining.

Jessica's eyes brightened. The thought of a cute new face around the office didn't exactly depress her, either. She was glad that she and Darcy saw eye to eye on love. She couldn't agree more that it was important to play the field. "Why do you think Eric's odd?" she asked

Darcy, returning to what the redhead had said a few moments earlier. "He strikes me as kind of shy."

"Yeah," Darcy agreed. "But he seems so jumpy whenever you ask him anything personal."

"That's true," Jessica conceded. "I thought that was the midwestern style, I guess. But you'd know much more about that than I would!"

Darcy snapped her fingers. "That reminds me! I was going to call my friend Sue in Cleveland and find out what she knows about Eric." She looked longingly at Jessica's phone. "Can I use your phone? I'll call collect. Sue's parents have lots of money—they won't mind."

"Sure," Jessica said. She wondered if Darcy still secretly liked Eric. Why waste time checking up on someone you didn't care about?

But then, Darcy was the kind of girl who liked to know everything about everyone, Jessica reminded herself as the redhead dialed Sue's number and asked the operator to make it a collect call. Within minutes she was filling her friend in on all the details about Eric Hankman.

"He didn't tell me which high school he went to, but I know he's from Shaker Heights. He's tall—about six feet—with dark brown hair. Eric

Hankman," Darcy told her friend. Jessica looked out the window, wishing Elizabeth would reappear with the Fiat. How her sister could spend this much time with Enid Rollins was beyond her!

"He's adorable, Sue. But I want to find out everything about him I can. Like, did he have a girlfriend in Shaker Heights? What kind of family is he from? You know how I am—I want to know everything!"

Sue must have gone into a whole long speech then, because Darcy just kept nodding and saying "Yeah" for about five minutes. Jessica was getting *really* bored.

"Come on, Darce. You can talk to her later," she finally urged.

But Darcy was transfixed, her eyes wide with horror. "You're kidding! When?" she kept shrieking. "Omigod! Oh, no!" Her face turned very pale, and despite herself Jessica got nervous. It seemed like an eternity before Darcy finally hung up. "Well, Sue has never heard of Eric," she announced, "but she's going to look into it. Anyway, something absolutely awful has happened since I left Ohio. About two weeks ago a girl in the town next to Sue's was murdered!" she exclaimed with a shudder. "God, Jess, it sounds so gruesome. She was exactly our age." Darcy covered her face with her hands. "They found her in a vacant lot—strangled. No one has any idea who could have done it."

"You're kidding," Jessica said, her eyes widening. She remembered that horrible moment earlier in the summer when she had seen the dead body in the Western Building parking lot. A visible shudder went through her.

"Sue says everyone in the whole town is up in arms. The girl was a model student, everyone knew her and liked her, and she was really pretty and everything. Sue didn't know her, but her sister did—they took a dance class together. Jess, isn't that awful?"

Jessica nodded. She was glad it had happened far away in Ohio.

"God," Darcy said, shaking her head. "And it was just before we moved out here."

Jessica took a deep breath. "Look, Darcy, do me a favor. Let's not talk about it right now."

Darcy shivered. "OK, Jess. I promise I won't mention it again." She was quiet for a minute. "Anyway, Sue said she'd try to find out some stuff for me about Eric. She hadn't heard of him, but she thought some of her sister's friends might know him."

Jessica nodded. She wasn't really concentrating on what Darcy was saying, though. She kept thinking about one thing—the girl in Ohio who was murdered.

Darcy, on the other hand, had recovered quickly. She strode over to Jessica's mirror and began to brush her hair. "I hope Andy turns out to be cute," she said. "If he is, will you help me get to know him better?"

Jessica laughed. "What about Eric?"

"Eric, too," Darcy said impulsively. Her eyes shone. "I want to get to know as many cute guys as I can. And I want you to help me!"

Seven

When Elizabeth woke up Sunday morning, she had a distinctly funny feeling, as if something were different, but she couldn't put her finger on it. Then memories of the night before came flooding back to her.

After their talk at Secca Lake, she and Eric had driven back into Sweet Valley for dinner. Eric insisted on treating Elizabeth, and they went to Guido's for pizza. They were both tired from their afternoon together, and it was a relief to relax in the pizza parlor and be more lighthearted.

"What I like about you, Elizabeth Wakefield, is that you can talk on so many different levels," Eric said after they had finished their pizza.

"On the one hand, you can be really serious. But you have a great sense of humor, and you can be really silly, too. Do you know how hard it is to find that in someone?"

Elizabeth felt suddenly shy. There was a certain way Eric looked at her that made her feel . . . She pushed the thought out of her mind. Eric was a new friend, and that was it. Period.

She dropped him off at home, and for a minute, just when he was fumbling with his seat belt, she thought things were going to get awkward. She was afraid he was going to try to kiss her good night. But instead he just turned to her, a sincere expression in his eyes. "This is one of the nicest days I've had in a long time," he told her. "Liz, I can't tell you how much it means to me being introduced to this beautiful town by someone as special as you."

"Thanks, Eric. I had fun," Elizabeth said, smiling.

"Will you let me reciprocate? Can I take you to a movie or something one night after work?"

Elizabeth couldn't help being glad that they would have a chance to spend more time together soon. "Why not?" she said with a smile.

"There's a new James Bond movie showing downtown. I passed by the theater the other day when I was going to work. Why don't we go together Monday night? We can grab a sand-wich from the coffee shop and make the seven o'clock show."

"That sounds great," Elizabeth told him.

Then she had driven home in a kind of rev-erie. She had never met anyone like Eric before. He seemed so intelligent, so sensitive. Now, as she lay in bed, she thought of the poem he had written titled "Harvest," and her eyes filled with tears as she thought about the hopelessness it gave voice to.

Poor Eric, she thought. Was it because his family had broken up that he was so sad, so mysterious?

Then she remembered the farewell poem. Who was the girl he'd written about? Elizabeth won-dered. Why did love necessarily have to "de-stroy"? Something about that poem had troubled her, though she couldn't put her finger on it. . . .

Suddenly Jessica burst through Elizabeth's bed-room door, dressed in jogging clothes and hold-ing her Walkman in her hand. "Aren't you up yet? Where were you last night? I was trapped here for *hours* waiting for the Fiat," she com-plained. "If Amy hadn't come over to rescue me, I would have gone crazy." She looked sus-piciously at her sister. "Why are you still in bed? What time did you get home, anyway?"

Elizabeth laughed at this interrogation. "I was

over at Enid's," she said. She felt bad about lying to Jessica, but she had decided to keep her friendship with Eric private, and letting her sister in on it was one way to guarantee it would be anything but!

Jessica wrinkled her nose. She thought Enid Rollins was boring and couldn't understand what her sister saw in her. "I'm going jogging," she announced, doing a few deep knee bends to warm up. "Want to get up and come with me?"

Elizabeth shook her head. "No," she said. "I'm going to write a letter to Jeffrey."

Jessica groaned. "First you spend a whole Saturday with Enid—keeping me from using the car, I might add—and then you waste a gorgeous Sunday morning inside writing to Jeffrey! Liz, I'll never understand you. Never!"

Elizabeth laughed at the mock-horror in Jessica's voice. Just then, she didn't particularly care whether Jessica understood her or not. She felt like being alone for a while to think about some of the things she and Eric had talked about. And she wanted to sort through her files. She had a few other stories she wanted Eric to see.

"OK," Darcy whispered to Jessica. It was Monday morning, and the two girls were downstairs in front of the coffee shop, trying to decide the best way to approach Eric.

"You should just go in and talk to him yourself," Jessica objected. "I told you what to say. Tell him you have two tickets to the Dodgers game tonight, and ask him if he wants to go. It's simple!"

Darcy frowned. "I just don't think that's the best technique with Eric. He's too shy. I think it'll work much better if he thinks I'm shy, too. So you go, and tell him I've got the tickets and want to take someone. Figure out a way to let him know how much I like him without making it seem like I'm too eager."

"All right," Jessica said with a sigh, "but I still think you ought to talk to him yourself."

Darcy shook her head. "Trust me, Jess. I know this kind of guy. I'll be waiting right down at the end of the hall. Come get me the *minute* you're done talking to him. And make it seem casual and natural, Jess. Don't make me look like an idiot."

"I'll do my best," Jessica said dryly. She opened the door to the coffee shop and strolled in. Eric looked up, gave her a big smile, then looked puzzled and glanced at her wrist.

"Oh—Jessica," he said, sounding disappointed. "Just a minute. Let me finish getting this order ready for the third floor." He was packing a cardboard box full of coffee cups.

Jessica tapped her fingers on the counter. "You look like you're getting used to this job," she remarked. She wished Darcy could do this on her own. She really didn't feel like going into a whole long song and dance about some stupid tickets to a ball game. Especially since Darcy's interests were more than a little divided. She seemed to like every boy she saw! But Darcy was a new friend, she reminded herself. And what else were friends for? Just this once she could do Darcy a favor.

"Yeah. Last week was pretty hectic, but now I think I've got things under control." Eric smiled at her. "What can I do for you?" he asked, once the box was packed up. "Don't tell me. You need coffee for one of those caffeine-freak reporters."

Jessica shook her head. "Just an orange juice. For Darcy," she said significantly. "That girl! I tried to get her to stop in and get some breakfast, but she's such a hard worker!" She watched Eric carefully out of the corner of her eye to see what his reaction was, but his expression didn't change.

"Seems like they're keeping all of you pretty busy up there," he said in a neutral voice. "I know your sister really seems to be working hard."

"Oh, Liz always works hard," Jessica said. "But Darcy . . . well, to tell you the truth, I'm a little bit worried about her, Eric. She hasn't taken a break in ages. And you know what it's like moving here from far away. In fact, you moved here from Ohio, too—right?"

"Right," Eric said, taking the orange juice out of a cooler.

Jessica slapped her hand to her forehead. "Gosh," she exclaimed with false surprise. "I forgot all about that! I bet you two have an awful lot to talk about, huh?"

Eric looked at Jessica closely. "Well, I guess so," he said awkwardly.

"You know," Jessica said conversationally, moving along the counter to stay near Eric while he poured the orange juice, "Darcy's dad said something this morning while he was driving us to work about having some extra tickets to the ball game tonight. Darcy's never been to a Dodgers game. Can you believe that?"

"Well, it makes sense—if she's just moved here," Eric said. He didn't seem to be exactly jumping for the bait.

"Anyway, he has two tickets," Jessica continued. "One for Darcy and one for a friend."

Eric raised his eyebrows, waiting.

"For tonight," Jessica added pointedly.

Eric put the orange juice in a paper bag. "That," he said, "comes to sixty-three cents, with tax."

Jessica fished around in her bag for some change. What was this guy's problem? Was she going to have to spell things out more clearly?

"Eric," she said, clearing her throat, "I think it would be awfully nice for Darcy if she had a break—after all this hard work lately. Maybe *you* could go with her to the game tonight."

"Me?" Eric seemed genuinely surprised.

"Yes, you," Jessica said firmly. "After all, you're both new in town. You're both from Ohio. And probably neither of you has ever seen a Dodgers game. What could be better?"

Eric looked embarrassed. "It's a nice idea, but actually I have plans tonight. I'm going to see the new James Bond movie."

Jessica bit her lip. This hadn't exactly gone as planned. She hoped Darcy would be a good sport about it, but something told her her new friend was going to have a fit. Darcy didn't seem like the type who took rejection well.

"Oh, well," she said casually, hoping her disappointment didn't show on her face. "Some other time, maybe. Thanks for the orange juice!"

She had barely made it halfway down the hall when Darcy rushed up to her. "What did he say? Did you ask him? Did you tell him about the tickets? Don't tell me!" she shrieked, covering her face with her hands. "He hates me! I can tell from your face."

Jessica chose her words carefully. "He doesn't hate you, Darce. Don't be crazy! But he's busy tonight." She handed Darcy the bag with the orange juice inside it. "He's going to the movies," she added, averting her eyes.

Darcy's eyes narrowed. "Fine," she snapped. "So he doesn't like me. See if I care!"

"Now, wait a minute, Darcy," Jessica said. "Maybe you should give him another chance. After all, you yourself pointed out how shy he is and everything. Just get to know him a little better. Meanwhile, there's always this new guy, Andy."

Darcy was inconsolable. "He hates me." She sighed. "Here I give him a perfectly wonderful chance to get to know me better, and he doesn't even take me up on it." She tossed back her hair. "Well, he'll come around. Just wait."

Jessica pushed the up button on the elevator. "I'm sure you're right," she said. Actually, judging from Eric's reaction, she couldn't imagine anything less likely. But she didn't want to get Darcy any angrier than she was.

Just then a tall, handsome boy with light brown, curly hair hurried into the elevator with them. He had sparkling gray-blue eyes, and in his navy blazer and khakis, he looked like the perfect picture of a college student ready for a summer job.

Darcy almost pounced, and Jessica had to hide her amusement. "What floor?" Darcy purred.

"Five," he said, smiling.

"Five?" Darcy acted as if it were the biggest coincidence on earth. "Why, that's our floor. You're not going up to the *News* office, are you?"

"Yeah, as a matter of fact, I am," he said, still smiling. "My name is Andy Sullivan. I'm going to be an intern at *The News* for the rest of the summer."

Darcy's face lit up, and Jessica hid a smile. Something told her that her new friend was going to get over her disappointment about Eric even faster than she'd expected.

"We're interns at *The News*, too!" Darcy exclaimed. By the time the elevator reached the fifth floor, she had told Andy more than he could possibly have wanted to hear about how excited she was to be working for a newspaper. Andy seemed friendly, but noncommittal.

"Well, I expect I'll see you girls later," he said when they reached the *News* office. "I'm supposed to go in and see Mr. Robb now."

Darcy glowed all over. "Jessica," she said, squeezing her friend's hand ecstatically, "I'm in love! Isn't he gorgeous?"

Jessica nodded. She didn't ask about Eric this time. It was better to leave well enough alone, she figured.

At least Darcy wasn't one to stay broken-hearted for long!

"Eric," Elizabeth said in a low voice. It was six-thirty, and they were walking together from the Western Building down Main Street toward the Valley Cinema. "Is it my imagination, or is that guy following us?"

Eric paled. "Which guy?" he demanded, spinning around.

"That guy in the gray suit," Elizabeth said in a low voice. She had noticed that the young man in the gray suit stopped when they stopped and started again when they did.

"Why would he follow us?" Eric said, looking anxiously back over his shoulder. He tried to act unconcerned, but it was clear he was worried. "Let's duck into the deli on the corner and see what he does."

Elizabeth nodded. She didn't know if she was just being paranoid, but she *did* think the man in the gray suit was behaving suspiciously.

"He's probably a friend of Darcy Kaymen's," Eric said with a nervous, tight-lipped smile when they were in the deli. "She wanted me to go to a ball game with her tonight. I don't think she's thrilled that I had other plans instead."

"He's going past," Elizabeth said with relief. "I guess I'm just paranoid. Sorry, Eric."

"I'll take care of you," he assured her. "You can count on that, Liz." Now that the man had passed, he seemed eager to brush the incident off, as if it hadn't mattered.

But Elizabeth could tell it had bothered him a great deal. As they walked toward the theater, Eric kept looking over his shoulder.

"Who would want to follow us, anyway?" Elizabeth joked when they got in line for tickets. "We've got to be about the last people in the world anyone would want to stalk."

Eric took his wallet out without a word. When Elizabeth looked closely at him, she saw beads of perspiration on his forehead. He was pale, and his fingers were trembling slightly.

For the dozenth time she found herself wondering why Eric was so nervous. He turned suddenly and gave her a penetrating look. "Does anyone know we're here together tonight?" he asked.

Elizabeth hesitated. The truth was, she had deliberately kept their date a secret. Mostly because she didn't want Jessica to find out. She didn't want her twin to get the wrong idea. She and Eric were just friends—nothing more. But she didn't want Jessica teasing her about it. "No," she murmured.

Eric swallowed. "Let's keep this our secret, all right?" he said, putting his arm around her. "It'll make our friendship even more special if no one knows you're meeting me. Is that OK with you?"

Elizabeth was astonished. Had he been reading her mind?

"But—why?" she wondered aloud. The fact that she herself preferred that no one find out was forgotten now that Eric seemed intent on the same end. Why wouldn't he want anyone to know?

"It's more romantic this way," he said. She couldn't see his expression, but she felt goose bumps rise on her arms. *More romantic.* Was that why she didn't want anyone—including Jeffrey—to know that she and Eric Hankman had been spending time together? She began to wonder if Eric wanted their friendship to turn into something more.

"That was great!" Eric said when they came out of the movie a few hours later. "That was just what I needed. Nothing like a good thriller to take your mind off things!"

What things? Elizabeth wondered. But she didn't want to press him. She knew Eric well enough now to realize that he hated being asked personal questions. Still, she wished he would open up to her more.

"Let's take a walk down on the beach. I love being so near the ocean," he said impetuously.

Elizabeth glanced at her watch. "I told my parents I'd be home by ten. It'll have to be a short walk," she said regretfully.

"That's OK." He put his arm around her and pulled her closer to him, and Elizabeth felt her stomach do a flip-flop. It was so good to be close to him, she thought. Just the touch of his arm made her feel breathless. And his warm breath against her hair . . . There was no denying that her pulse was racing. She could barely swallow as she turned to face him.

"Uh—we should get your car," she said, pulling away and walking in the direction of the Western Building garage. She didn't like the way she was feeling at all. What was wrong with her, anyway? she scolded herself. She was in love with Jeffrey. Why did her pulse quicken when another guy touched her?

They drove in silence to the beach. On her part, Elizabeth felt the silence was tense. She was thinking about a million things. What about Jeffrey? What did it mean that she enjoyed another boy's company so much? What about the way it felt when Eric's hand brushed hers? Her lips burned as she imagined kissing him. She felt terrible—confused, uncertain, guilty. And at the same time she felt exhilarated to be driving with Eric toward the ocean, just the two of them. Her mind was in a turmoil. With an effort, she tried to make conversation.

"Have you been writing more poetry?" she asked him when they parked by the beach and got out of the car. She realized even as she asked this question that it was her way of trying to find out more about what he was thinking and feeling. Tacitly, they had allowed their writing—his poems and her stories—to be the vehicle for their emotions. It was the only way to ask Eric a direct question without angering him.

He was quiet for a minute. "Actually, I have," he admitted. "Liz, have you ever read any of Petrarch's poems?"

Elizabeth shook her head. "Who's Petrarch? Sorry if that's ignorant, but I don't know anything about him."

"An Italian poet. He lived a long time ago—in the fourteenth century. He wrote the most beautiful love poems," Eric said softly. "He met a girl named Laura and fell madly in love with her and wrote this beautiful series of poems to her—three hundred sixty-six of them, one for each day of the year and then one extra. Like forever and a day," he mused.

Elizabeth looked up at the moon and shivered. It was so beautiful here by the water.

"I've been writing love poems, too," Eric said then. He looked straight at Elizabeth, his eyes very big and serious.

Elizabeth felt her heart pound. She didn't want him to say anything more. The minute he did, the delicate balance between them would be ruined. She would have to tell him about Jeffrey—she would have to explain so many things and try to figure out so much.

This way, before anything had been said directly, there was something magical between them. She knew then, looking up at Eric's strong, handsome face, exactly what he was feeling.

"Shhh," she said when he started to speak again. She put her finger up against his lips, and he kissed it.

"There's so much I want to say to you, Liz," he protested.

Elizabeth shook her head. "Not now. Not yet," she whispered.

She knew this delicate balance wasn't going

to last. But she wanted to hold on to it as long as possible.

She was frightened again as she looked up at his face. And not just because he was awakening feelings in her that she wished weren't there.

Something about that shadow that crossed his face . . . she found herself wanting to cry out with frustration. Who was this guy? Why did he have such a strong hold over her? And why was he so secretive?

Part of her wanted to find out all she could about Eric Hankman. And the other part didn't care. She just wanted to stay with him there forever.

Eight

Tuesday morning Darcy was at work at least half an hour before anyone else arrived, straightening up her desk, arranging things so she looked both busy and neat at the same time. She had taken special pains with her appearance that morning and could hardly wait until Jessica showed up so she could ask her new friend's advice on how to win over Andy Sullivan. She had lots of ideas herself, but there was no point leaving anything to chance! She had already sneaked a peak at his resumé, which she'd found on Mr. Robb's desk. Not surprisingly, Andy was as perfect on paper as he seemed in person. Straight A's. Varsity basketball. Junior editor of *The Stanford Daily*. All sorts of honors and awards for sports, scholastics, writing. "Just my sort of man," Darcy said to herself with a little smile.

Jessica arrived at nine o'clock, and Darcy practically assaulted her. "Come in here," she cried, dragging Jessica into the library and closing the door firmly behind her. "We've got to talk strategy. Jess, you have to help me plan!"

"Plan what?" Jessica asked, yawning. Mornings had never been Jessica's favorite part of the day.

"Plan how to get Andy to notice me. I mean, I'm sure he's already *noticed* me," Darcy amended hastily. "But I mean really and truly realize that I'm the one."

Jessica laughed. "Is this the same girl who wanted Eric Hankman to go to the baseball game with her last night?" she teased.

But Darcy couldn't be teased. "I like Eric," she said with a pout. "In fact, if it weren't for Andy, I'd be really upset about Eric, Jess. You should be more sensitive."

"Sorry," Jessica said, hiding her mirth. "OK. So what's the game plan for Andy?" Her eyes sparkled. "Is it my imagination, or am I going to have something to do with it?"

Darcy looked anxiously through the glass window of the library door. "He's here!" she exclaimed. "I'm going to offer to buy him a cup of coffee. How's that for a first move?"

"Sounds good to me." Jessica smiled. Poor Andy, she was thinking. He didn't know what was about to hit him!

"How do I look?" Darcy asked anxiously, pivoting to show Jessica the green knit dress she had bought on the way home from work the night before.

Jessica studied her critically. "You look great. I like that dress a lot," she said.

"You're sure I don't look a little—you know—voluptuous?" Darcy worried.

She *did* have a pretty curvy figure, but Jessica honestly had to admit she thought the redhead looked sensational. "You look wonderful," Jessica said.

Darcy smiled. "Well, wish me luck! I don't even think I'll ask him first if he wants coffee. I'll just bring him a cup, sort of like it's just an accident," she added, opening the door and peering around outside. The coast seemed to be clear, and she ducked out into the hallway.

Darcy hurried out to the elevator banks, passing Elizabeth on her way.

"Hi," Elizabeth said, smiling at her.

Darcy gave her a silent stare. "Excuse me," she said, brushing past Elizabeth into the elevator. She could feel Elizabeth looking after her, but she didn't care. Elizabeth was far too serious for Darcy's tastes. She wished Elizabeth would lighten up about working at *The News* for the summer. Darcy knew that Elizabeth wanted to write professionally and that she viewed her summer internship as a move in that direction, but her earnestness in the office just made it more difficult for Darcy to have some fun; that was why Darcy had pulled all those little tricks on Elizabeth. Now Darcy stared straight ahead as the elevator doors closed, not paying the slightest bit of attention to Elizabeth's look of hurt and consternation.

The coffee shop was empty when Darcy swept in. Eric was sitting at one of the tables, intent on something he was writing in a blue spiral notebook.

"Hi, Eric!" Darcy said sunnily. She sat down across from him at the table. "Not very busy in here, is it?" She had forgotten how cute he was. For just a minute she wondered . . . But no, Andy was much more interesting—older, more mature. Still, it was kind of a shame about Eric. She gave him a flirtatious look just for old time's sake.

"No," Eric said with a stiff smile, closing the notebook. "The big rush is between eight and nine, then it slows down."

Darcy fiddled with her bracelet. "You know, Eric," she said in a coy voice, "I was pretty disappointed when Jessica told me that you couldn't come with me to the game last night. In fact, I had to invite the son of one of my father's business partners—Ted McCarthy. I think Ted really likes me," she added silkily. The truth was that Darcy hadn't gone to the game at all. But she didn't want Eric to know that.

"That sounds like fun," Eric murmured.

Darcy shot him a look. It bothered her that Eric didn't seem upset—even though she was really interested in Andy. She decided to see what kind of reaction she could get out of Eric if she really tried hard. "But I was really thinking about *you* all night," she continued. She leaned forward, edging her fingers toward his.

Eric looked at her with alarm. "Uh—why?" he managed.

"What do you mean, why?" Darcy demanded. "Eric, don't you realize—"

Unfortunately, the door to the coffee shop opened just then, and a customer came in. Eric jumped up right away, looking grateful, and hurried over to the counter. Darcy drummed her fingers on the table waiting for him to come back. She couldn't resist taking a little peek inside his notebook while he was away. It was just an ordinary blue spiral notebook, with Eric's name and address printed neatly on the inside cover. She was just turning to examine the first page when Eric came back like a shot, tearing the notebook from her.

"Don't!" he snapped. He seemed embarrassed by the strength of his response and added, more gently, "Sorry, I'm just kind of private about this." He clutched the notebook to him. "It's poetry, and I feel funny about letting anyone read it."

Darcy's eyes brightened. "What kind of poetry? Love poetry?" she asked meaningfully.

Eric turned bright red. "Sort of," he muttered, looking completely mortified.

"Who's it written to?" Darcy demanded.

Eric stared at her. "Uh . . . well, no one. I mean—" He shifted uncomfortably, and Darcy narrowed her eyes.

"It has to be for someone, if it's love poetry," she pointed out. She gave him an especially coy smile. "It's for me, isn't it?" she demanded.

Eric bit his lip and was silent for a moment. "Yeah," he said finally, swallowing hard. "It is. But, Dar—"

She didn't let him finish. "Don't worry," she said soothingly. She felt a rush of sympathy for him now. Just when he realized how much he cared for her, she had met another man!

Darcy felt a twinge of regret, but only a twinge. After all, these things happened. Painful as it would be for Eric, he would have to get over her—somehow. Meanwhile, Darcy intended to bask in his attention. Maybe she could even use him to make Andy Sullivan pay more attention to her!

Another customer came in, and Eric went over to the counter, taking the notebook with him. But Darcy wasn't about to be outfoxed now that she knew there were poems in that notebook—poems about her. She watched Eric set it down and waited until he was engrossed in filling the customer's order before she raced over to the counter and scooped up the book.

"Darcy!" Eric cried. "Excuse me," he said to the customer, "but I—"

But it was too late. Darcy had already managed to tear out the first page in the notebook. The first part of a poem, printed neatly in Eric's small firm writing, began "To Her—" Darcy didn't know much about poetry, but she didn't care. A poem, written about her! Her eyes were bright with excitement.

"I know you really meant for me to have this anyway," she whispered conspiratorially to Eric. "I'll see you later, OK? Write me another one, and bring it up to the office! Oh, and can I have a cup of coffee, please? Just black. I'll take the cream and sugar on the side."

Eric stared at her. He had no choice but to do what she asked. And he couldn't attempt to retrieve the poem—the customer was still waiting for his coffee. Eric got the coffee for Darcy, and she raced out the door before he could stop her, the poem—and Andy's cup of coffee— securely in her hands.

"Well," Darcy announced at lunchtime, taking her ham-and-cheese sandwich out of her bag, "the old expression is true. It never rains but it pours. Yesterday I didn't think I'd ever find a guy who really cares about me. And now Andy and Eric are practically fighting over me!"

Elizabeth, Jessica, and Darcy were eating lunch together in the library, the door closed so they could have some privacy. Elizabeth looked at Darcy with alarm. What did she mean about Eric fighting over her?

Jessica raised her eyebrows. "You're kidding. Since when? I thought Eric was—you know, kind of cool."

"He was," Darcy admitted. "In fact, I'd pretty much given up on him till this morning. I went down to get coffee for Andy, and Eric was sitting there writing something in a notebook.

Naturally I asked him what it was." She leaned forward, lowering her voice. "You'll never believe it. It turns out it was love poetry. I still didn't think it was such a big deal. But when I kind of teased him about it, he told me. It was for *me!*" She glowed with pleasure. "I managed to swipe one of the poems," she added. "I figure I can let Andy just *find* it. You know how it works. One guy finds out another one likes you, and you're suddenly about a billion times more interesting."

Elizabeth put her sandwich down. She didn't have much of an appetite anymore.

Jessica couldn't hide her surprise. "Wow. I really misjudged that one," she said. "Let me see the poem."

Darcy produced the sheet of paper, well-worn now from her close examination.

Jessica read it with fascination. "I can't believe it! And just yesterday he seemed so— uninterested. What do you think happened between then and now?"

Darcy shrugged. "I think he just realized his true feelings, that's all." She took the poem back and looked at it with satisfaction. "Actually, just between us, I think there's something a little funny about Eric. I can't wait to call Sue back and see if she's found out anything more about him. Anyway, I'm glad I'm over him," she declared. "Andy's much more pulled together in every way." She giggled. "But I have to admit I'm kind of flattered!"

Elizabeth was aghast. She had listened so far in complete silence, feeling worse and worse. How on earth could Eric have written a poem for Darcy? Elizabeth wondered if all those things he had said to her were just pure nonsense. She felt horrible.

"Can I see that poem?" she asked Darcy, trying to keep the distress out of her voice.

"Sure," Darcy said. "Only be careful. It's precious," she added, passing it to Elizabeth. "And don't let Eric know I showed it to you. He's really sensitive about people reading his poetry without asking him first."

Elizabeth stared at her but didn't say anything. She picked up the piece of paper. "To Her," she read. It was unmistakably Eric's printing.

She could barely focus on the words below. So Eric really *had* written a love poem to Darcy. She felt terrible. How could he? What about everything he'd said the day before to her? Didn't it mean anything?

Feeling distraught, Elizabeth pushed the poem away. "Excuse me," she said, getting to her feet. She couldn't stand being around Darcy just then, and she didn't care if her expression gave her away.

She just wanted to be alone. She had a lot of thinking to do. And she certainly couldn't do it in front of Darcy, especially now!

By Tuesday evening Elizabeth was in a terrible state about Eric. She had thought about nothing else all day and had deliberately avoided him, going out by a different exit so she wouldn't have to walk past the coffee shop and run into him. Every time she imagined him with Darcy she got more upset. And not just because she didn't like the thought of Eric being interested in Darcy, though that was certainly most of it. Elizabeth was also upset because her own reaction was so strong, and that meant facing up to the fact that she must have some feelings for Eric that went beyond mere friendship.

At dinner Elizabeth could tell her bad mood showed, and she wasn't doing much to try to hide it.

"Honey, can you toss the salad for me?" Mrs. Wakefield asked her.

Elizabeth sighed heavily as she crossed the kitchen.

"Is anything wrong?" her mother asked.

"No. Just a long day," Elizabeth said. She kept thinking about the poem, "To Her." The thought of Eric actually writing *Darcy* a poem!

"What is it, Liz?" her mother asked again, twenty minutes later, when the family and Adam were sitting down together for dinner. "You haven't even touched your food."

"I'm sorry, Mom. It's delicious. I'm just tired, I guess."

Mr. Wakefield looked thoughtfully at her. "Liz, have you gotten to be friendly with Eric Hankman since he and his father moved here? I've been helping Rich Hankman with a business contract, and he mentioned that Eric has brought your name up several times."

Elizabeth reddened. Why did her father have to bring Eric up now? She remembered the promise she and Eric had made to each other to keep their friendship secret. But she didn't like to lie to her parents. She decided to play down the truth.

"Pretty friendly, I guess. We say hello to each other and talk a little bit at work." Jessica was staring at her across the table. The fact that Elizabeth had anything to do with Eric was clearly news to her. And from the look on her face, it was something she wanted to hear more about.

"Well, Mr. Hankman says that Eric's been raving about you." Mr. Wakefield smiled at her. "He seems to be a really nice guy from everything his father says. Rich is an interesting man," he added, turning to Mrs. Wakefield. "I like him quite a bit. In fact, I suggested they both come over here on Friday night for a barbecue."

"That sounds nice," Mrs. Wakefield said. "Especially if Liz and Eric are already friends. It's OK with you, isn't it, Liz?"

"Oh, it's fine," Elizabeth muttered, staring down at her plate. "Just fine."

She listened without appetite while her father went on describing how Mr. Hankman was a private businessman who had decided opportunities for growth were much better here in California. Mr. Wakefield, who didn't usually handle contracts, had taken care of Mr. Hankman for one of his partners, who was currently out of town.

Elizabeth picked absently at her food, thinking what awful timing it was that her father had lit on the idea of having the Hankmans over *now*. Maybe they should invite Darcy, too, she thought.

She could barely wait until dinner was over and she could escape to her room to be alone.

"OK," Jessica said, opening Elizabeth's door without bothering to knock first. "Would you mind telling me what's going on?"

"What do you mean?" Elizabeth said. "And,

Jess, since when do you barge in here without knocking?"

"Since when do you get so friendly with some guy without telling me about it?" Jessica demanded indignantly.

"I haven't. It's nothing. Eric is just a friend," Elizabeth said hotly.

"That's what I thought. So why are you getting so upset about the whole thing? What's the big deal if Mom and Dad have him and his father over for a barbecue?"

"There isn't any big deal. Jess, would you do me a favor and just leave me alone?" Elizabeth cried.

Jessica stared at her. "You know, Liz, if I didn't know any better, I'd think there was something awfully peculiar about the way you're acting. You seem a little too moody for someone who's 'just friends' with Eric Hankman."

"Cut it out, Jess," Elizabeth warned. "I mean it. I want to be alone."

"OK, OK," Jessica said, backing out and pulling the door closed behind her. "Boy," she added out loud, "aren't *we* in a good mood!"

Elizabeth ignored this comment. She stared forlornly out the window, wondering why she was behaving so horrendously.

The truth was, she knew the answer. Elizabeth felt that she had started to fall in love with

Eric. Where that left her, she had no idea. Apart from anything else, she knew she had some tough things to confront about her innermost feelings for Jeffrey.

Even worse, Eric had written that poem to Darcy. All those things he had said to Elizabeth the night before had obviously just been flirtatious banter. She had a hard time imagining Eric was the sort of guy who could be so callous, but how else would Darcy have managed to get that poem in her possession?

Nine

"Jessica!" Darcy's eyes were wide with excitement. "I absolutely *have* to talk to you. Can we go somewhere where no one can hear us?"

It was Wednesday morning, and Jessica had just gotten to the *News* office, where she found Darcy—looking even more excited and anxious than usual—waiting for her right by the front door.

"Sure," Jessica said. "Let's go in the library and shut the door."

Darcy shook her head. "Not private enough," she said. "Why don't we tell Dan we're going out for coffee? Then we can find someplace where no one can hear us."

"This isn't just another excuse to spend more time in the coffee shop, is it?" Jessica teased her.

"No! Come on, Jess," Darcy pleaded.

Jessica relented, and soon the two girls had slipped downstairs and outside.

"Hey!" Seth called, spotting them on his way in. "Aren't you two heading in the wrong direction?"

"We're running an errand," Jessica blurted out. "We'll be back in a second, Seth!" To Darcy she added, under her breath, "Darcy, this better be good!"

"Listen, Jess," the girl said, grabbing Jessica's arm, "I talked to my friend Sue last night. Something really strange is going on, and I've just got to tell someone about it. Remember I told you about that girl who was murdered?"

Jessica nodded. "I remember. What about it?"

By now the two girls had crossed the busy street in front of the Western Building, and Darcy gestured for Jessica to follow her. She led her into the diner on the corner, which was busy with early morning customers. "This should be safe." Darcy sat down at an empty table in the corner, and Jessica joined her, feeling confused.

"Look, why all the mystery?" she demanded. "What did Sue tell you?"

"Well," Darcy said, dropping her voice, "it looks like the girl was killed by someone she went out with a couple of times. The whole thing's pretty grisly, but Sue says no one in Ohio is talking about anything else. The police are trying to find the guy now, but they think he may have skipped town." Darcy's eyes were wide with excitement. "They don't know where he is. He could be *anywhere*."

Jessica shrugged. "It's a horrible story," she conceded, "but I don't really see—"

"Look," Darcy said, lowering her voice and glancing around to make sure no one was listening in on their conversation. "According to Sue, this girl was killed exactly four days before Eric Hankman first moved to Sweet Valley."

Jessica stared at her. "You're not saying—"

"And," Darcy added, putting her hands on the table and staring at Jessica with a look of terror in her eyes, "Eric fits the description Sue says the police are giving: seventeen years old, dark hair, hazel eyes, a sort of shifty, mysterious look. . . ."

Jessica couldn't believe what she was hearing. A shudder passed through her as she remembered what Darcy had said before about the girl who had been murdered. "What else do they know about this guy?" Jessica asked in a low, choked voice.

"Not a whole lot," Darcy said. "Apparently the Ohio police have linked this girl's murder with a similar case that occurred last fall. The police think the murderer is a psychopath who forms relationships with girls and then kills them." She shuddered. "It's just too awful," she moaned. "Jess, we have to find out everything we can about Eric. And I mean *everything*."

Jessica was beginning to get upset. "Eric *is* kind of weird," she whispered. "He gets that really strange look in his eyes every once in a while." She gripped the sides of the table. "Tell me what else Sue said."

"Not much." Darcy shook her head. "Except that there are lots of police working on the case. They're worried that the killer will strike again—and soon!"

Jessica grimaced. "It's pretty horrible," she said. Even sitting in the brightly lit diner, hundreds and hundreds of miles from the scene of the crime, she felt a shiver run down her spine as she imagined what this boy must be like. She gulped. "Darcy, you don't really think that Eric—"

Darcy's eyes were huge. "All I'm saying," she said in a low voice, "is that we have to watch him, Jess. Watch every move he makes. And we'll both report to each other anything we see that looks out of the ordinary. OK?"

Jessica nodded. "Do you think we should tell someone? Like my dad or maybe Mr. Robb?"

Darcy looked horrified. "No way, Jess. Be real! The whole point is that we have an advantage because Eric won't try to act different in front of us. He'll have no way of knowing we know. No, we just have to act normal and watch him—for now."

Jessica nodded. "All right," she said. But the thought didn't exactly thrill her.

"Good! Now remember, watch for *any* kind of suspicious behavior, and I will, too. Then we can compare notes."

Jessica got to her feet. "Wow," she said, under her breath. "Good thing you didn't go to the game with him on Monday night!" Her eyes widened. "Oh, no! he's coming over to our house on Friday for dinner!" She clutched Darcy's arm.

Darcy looked scornful. "Jess, don't overreact. He's not going to go running around with a machete or anything. The point is, just *watch* him. It's good he's coming over to your house. It'll mean you can really get a good look at how he's behaving."

Jessica nodded. Darcy was probably right. But all the same, just thinking about Eric Hankman right now made her shiver. How on earth was she going to pretend everything was normal when she saw him in the Western Building, let alone at their house on Friday night?

With a little effort, Elizabeth managed to avoid Eric all day Wednesday. It wasn't hard: she entered the building through the side entrance, didn't go down to the coffee shop, and stayed at work late on Wednesday evening.

If only keeping Eric out of her thoughts were as easy!

Ever since Elizabeth had seen the poem, she felt terrible. To think she had actually begun to believe he really cared about her, that she was something special to him! She should have known better. Hadn't he given her all sorts of signs that there was something peculiar going on—his secretiveness, his reluctance to open up to her? What she had assumed stemmed from a painful childhood must actually have been a natural reluctance to share private feelings with a girl he wasn't that close to. Elizabeth felt hurt and angry. She was determined to stay out of Eric's way until she had forgotten the whole incident.

In fact, when Jessica grilled her about Eric on Wednesday night, Elizabeth was able to tell her quite truthfully that she intended to have nothing to do with him.

"Good," Jessica had said with visible relief. "Because Darcy—"

At that, Elizabeth had lost her temper. "Look, Jess," she had fumed. "I've tried to be patient, but I just don't like that girl. I don't want to hear anything about her!" And she had slammed her door shut with uncharacteristic force.

Deep down Elizabeth knew she was reacting so strongly only because she cared so much. But she wasn't going to admit that to anyone— least of all to Jessica. Jessica knew nothing about her friendship with Eric, and Elizabeth intended to keep it that way!

But on Thursday morning Seth asked Elizabeth to run down and get him some coffee. There was no avoiding the situation any longer. She would have to confront Eric.

Luckily, there were several other customers in the shop, and Elizabeth, refusing to meet Eric's gaze, simply asked for a cup of coffee.

"I've been looking for you everywhere," Eric said under his breath so the other customers wouldn't hear. "Where have you been?"

"And a doughnut," Elizabeth said, still not looking at him.

"Liz!" Eric cried, anguished. The customer behind Elizabeth coughed, and Eric sighed. He had no choice but to fill her order in silence.

But she had underestimated him. She was

walking toward the elevator, the brown bag in her hand, when she heard footsteps running up behind her.

It was Eric, red-faced and out of breath.

"Why have you been avoiding me?" he demanded. His eyes, fixed intently on hers, were full of hurt.

Elizabeth gave him a cold look. "Why should I avoid you?" she asked. To keep her expression hard she had only to remind herself how she had felt when she'd seen that poem in Darcy's hand.

"I happen to care a lot about you, Liz," Eric said, sounding anguished. "I thought you cared, too. Now I try to talk to you, and you act like we're total strangers. You order coffee from me as if I'm just *anybody*. What's up, Liz? Why the silent treatment? If I did something to upset you I want to hear about it directly."

Elizabeth softened a little. "You're right, I should've just come right out and told you. But I felt embarrassed. The truth is, Eric, I liked *you* a lot, too." She looked away from his gaze, which was almost too intense to bear.

"Then Darcy showed me that poem you wrote her, and I guess my feelings were hurt," Elizabeth continued.

Eric stared at her. "You mean that's what this whole thing is about? That poem?"

Elizabeth glared at him. So it was true! "That poem," she mimicked, "happens to have made me feel pretty awful, Eric. If I'd known you write poems for every single girl you ever meet—" She broke off. Already she had revealed more than she intended to.

Eric looked at her beseechingly. "Look, Liz. I didn't really write it for Darcy. I just told her that because—" Now it was his turn to break off and look embarrassed. "I guess because I didn't want anyone to know that it was for you. That seems like—you know, part of our secret." He touched her hand imploringly. "Please try to understand. I didn't want to tell Darcy who it was really for. And I had no idea she'd ever tell you about it! Otherwise . . ."

Elizabeth swallowed hard. "It was really for me, then?" she managed to say.

Eric nodded. "Of course it was, Liz."

The two of them stared at each other for a long, tense moment. Then Elizabeth relented, and she smiled. "I guess it was silly of me to get so mad," she murmured.

Eric shook his head. His eyes darkened momentarily. "I don't blame you," he said. "If I thought—" He stopped short. "Liz, if there was someone else in your life, I don't know what I'd do!" he cried.

Elizabeth stared at him, a feeling of horror

coming over her as she realized what he meant. Why hadn't it occurred to her that he might feel this way? And what on earth would she do if he found out about Jeffrey?

Her hurt and anger had disappeared, and all she felt now was profound confusion. She had to figure out how she felt about Eric—fast. Because she was going to have to tell him the truth about Jeffrey—before someone else did.

Friday evening Mr. Wakefield got home early to help Mrs. Wakefield get ready for the barbecue. "I spoke to Rich Hankman, and he said he and his son will be over around seven-thirty," he said, giving his wife a kiss. "Oh, and I asked the Beckwiths to come, too. Is that all right with you?"

The Beckwiths were neighbors of the Wakefields and were often included in casual get-togethers. Mr. Beckwith was an insurance agent who worked in the Western Building. "That's fine," Mrs. Wakefield said, forming the hamburger patties."

Jessica wandered in and helped herself to a handful of potato chips. "What time is everyone coming? I'm starved!" She was proud of how casual she sounded. No one would know that she had just hung up the phone from a long strategy session with Darcy. They had decided exactly what things Jessica should be on the lookout for in Eric's behavior. *What an actress,* Jessica praised herself. She helped herself to more chips.

The phone rang, and Mrs. Wakefield looked helplessly down at her messy fingers. "Jess, can you grab it?"

But asking Jessica to answer the phone was never necessary. She was already at the receiver. "Oh, hi, Darcy," she said.

"Listen," Darcy hissed, "I'm sorry to be such a pest, but I just had a call from Sue. She says there was a whole long story in the paper today about you-know-what." Darcy's voice dropped conspiratorially. "Is he there yet?"

"Nope," Jessica said, her eye on her mother.

"Remember, anything out of the ordinary. Watch him like a hawk," Darcy said. "Especially look for dramatic mood swings. According to the psychologist they've put on the case, that's one of this guy's chief characteristics."

"OK," Jessica said, still watching her mother. She didn't want her parents or Elizabeth to know what was going on. "Look, I'll talk to you later," she said.

Darcy sounded nervous. "Be careful," she warned before hanging up. Jessica felt a shiver run through her.

The closer it got to seven-thirty—the time the Hankmans were due to arrive—the more jittery Jessica felt. She kept imagining horrible scenarios in which Eric got angry and turned into a raving psychopath. The more she thought about it, the more she was sure Eric was the murderer being sought by the Ohio police. He certainly seemed to go through mood swings. And that dark, stormy look he got in his eyes sometimes . . . It was all Jessica could do to sit calmly with Steven and Adam outside, waiting for the barbecue to get started. The Beckwiths arrived early, and soon Jessica, Adam, and Steven were sitting outside with them on the patio drinking iced tea and waiting for the Hankmans.

"Where's Liz?" Steven asked.

Jessica frowned. It wasn't like Elizabeth to spend this much time getting ready for dinner. She decided to go upstairs to see what was going on.

"Liz," she said, standing in the doorway of the bathroom watching her twin apply mascara. "Why are you so dressed up?"

"I'm not dressed up," Elizabeth said defensively. "This is just an old skirt, Jess."

Jessica frowned. "And why are you putting on makeup? It's only a family barbecue, Liz." Her eyes narrowed. "You're not trying to look better for Eric's sake, I hope. Because—"

Elizabeth cut her off. "Look," she said calmly, "I'm not trying to look better for anyone's sake but my own. Now cut it out, Jess."

"Liz, there's something I have to tell you about Eric," Jessica said, dead serious.

But Elizabeth refused to listen. "I don't want to hear you say *one* thing about him," she cried. "I mean it!"

Jessica had never heard her sister sound so insistent, and she realized she had better drop the subject. "Just promise me that you and Eric aren't friends—that you'd never go with him anywhere or do anything with him," Jessica said frantically. Her sister's safety was far more important than anything else; it was worth risking her anger for!

To Jessica's relief, Elizabeth smiled. "Jessica, Eric and I have never done more than say hello at work," she said. "And it's going to stay that way."

"OK," Jessica said, mollified. She turned to go downstairs. *Thank heavens for that,* she thought. All she needed was for Elizabeth to fall for some kind of psychopath! It was bad enough that her parents had actually invited him into their house.

Elizabeth walked out to the patio a minute later, looking slightly flustered—probably due to their talk, Jessica thought.

"Have some iced tea, dear," Mrs. Wakefield said.

Elizabeth greeted Mr. and Mrs. Beckwith politely and poured herself a glass. Just then the door bell rang, and she jumped up, spilling some of the iced tea on her skirt.

"Darn it," she muttered.

"I'll get it, Liz. Just relax," Mrs. Wakefield said, giving her a pat on the shoulder. Frowning, Jessica watched her sister. She was about to say something to her when she remembered that her role for the evening was to watch Eric's behavior, not her sister's. And anyway, Mr. Hankman and Eric were coming out on the patio behind Mrs. Wakefield, waiting to be introduced.

Jessica had to admit Eric looked like anything but a psychopath. He was wearing gray cotton pants and a faded polo shirt, and he looked happy to be there, if a little shy. Not exactly like a murderer. But wasn't the whole point that this guy looked clean-cut and respectable enough to make nice girls fall in love with him? Jessica shuddered.

"OK, time for introductions. Dan and Amy Beckwith, I'd like you to meet Rich Hankman and his son Eric. The Beckwiths live next door," Mrs. Wakefield said with a smile.

"Pleased to meet you," Mr. Beckwith said,

reaching out to shake hands with father and son.

"And this is Adam Maitland, a friend of Steven's who's living with us this summer. Steven—Jessica—Elizabeth . . ."

Elizabeth got awkwardly to her feet, her face pink.

But Jessica wasn't looking at her sister. She was too busy concentrating on Eric, who struck her as distinctly ill-at-ease. He mumbled when he shook hands with Mr. Wakefield and wouldn't look Mrs. Wakefield in the eye.

"Rich Hankman," Mr. Beckwith murmured with a frown. "No," he said finally, "the name doesn't ring a bell. But I never forget a face," he added, "and yours sure looks familiar. Have you and I met somewhere before?"

"I don't think so," Mr. Hankman said with a polite smile. "At least I can't think where."

"Hankman, Hankman, Hankman," Mr. Beckwith murmured. He frowned. "Did you go to Cornell, by any chance?"

"No," Mr. Hankman demurred, "I'm afraid not. I studied in Chicago. I'm a midwesterner through and through."

Just then Eric knocked over the glass of iced tea on the table beside him. His face turned scarlet as the drink spilled all over the patio floor.

"Gosh, I'm sorry," he gasped.

Mrs. Wakefield hurried to wipe up the spill. "Don't worry," she reassured him. "We all seem to be losing our grip on these glasses tonight!"

Jessica narrowed her eyes at Eric. Clearly he didn't want to talk about the Midwest. Who could blame him? He obviously wouldn't want to talk about Ohio if he and his father were trying to forget everything about what had happened to him there.

"Well, who would like to be the first in line for a hamburger?" Mrs. Wakefield asked.

Steven raised his hand. "Me!" he cried, and everyone laughed. Even at eighteen Steven's appetite was like that of a growing boy, and the family often teased him about it.

Soon everyone had food, and the group was sitting around the patio tables out on the Wakefields' deck. "It's awfully kind of you to have us over here," Mr. Hankman said, giving Mrs. Wakefield a warm smile. "It's tough being new in town. We really appreciate your hospitality."

Jessica, ignoring her food, was staring at Eric. She could imagine just how tough it was, if everything Darcy suspected was true.

"This is a hospitable town, Rich," Mr. Wakefield said with a smile. "Give us a chance, and you'll wish you had your privacy back. You won't find friendlier people anywhere."

Mr. Beckwith set down his hamburger. "I hate to keep saying so, but you really look familiar to me, Rich. You can't think of any place where we would've met?"

"No," Mr. Hankman said, still pleasantly, but with a firmness that made it seem pointless to continue the discussion.

Jessica was riveted. This was exactly the kind of thing Darcy had warned her about! It was obvious that Mr. Hankman was trying to protect his son. He didn't want to talk about the past.

But Mr. Beckwith was persistent. "Let's see," he continued. "I've never spent any time in Chicago, so that's not a possibility. Have you ever done any business on the West Coast? Ever been to graduate school out here or anything?"

"No," Mr. Hankman said. He was starting to look uncomfortable.

"Maybe our sons know each other." Mr. Beckwith smiled at Eric. "I've got a son a couple of years older than you. He's working in San Francisco this summer. His name is Jack. Jack Beckwith? Ever met him?"

"No," Eric said. He glanced at his father. Both father and son were looking stiff and uncomfortable now.

Right, Jessica thought. *You're hitting a nerve now.* If Eric looked familiar, Mr. Hankman didn't want him to figure out why. Who would—with a killer for a son? She shivered.

"Sometimes people just look familiar, honey," Mrs. Beckwith said with a smile.

Everyone looked at Mr. Hankman. He was an attractive man in his early fifties, a little on the portly side, with dark hair, glasses, and a salt-and-pepper beard.

Jessica turned her attention to Eric. He seemed more than a little nervous. He kept glancing anxiously at his father and seemed uncomfortable whenever Mr. Beckwith scrutinized him or asked him a direct question.

Jessica felt a fluttery, anxious feeling in her stomach. She could barely look at Eric without feeling choked up with fear. She couldn't wait until the Hankmans were gone.

And as it turned out, she didn't have to wait long. Shortly after dinner Mr. Hankman announced apologetically, that he had to get home early. Eric, looking ill-at-ease and unhappy, got to his feet when his father did.

"It's been a real pleasure," Mr. Hankman said warmly, shaking hands all around. He paused slightly when he got to Mr. Beckwith. "And a pleasure meeting you, too, Dan. Maybe we'll figure out yet what our connection is." He laughed, but the laugh struck Jessica as distinctly strained.

"Good night," Eric murmured to Elizabeth, giving her hand a squeeze.

Jessica's eyes were fixed suspiciously on him. Fortunately, Elizabeth didn't seem to register any emotion in her face as he left. She was obviously telling the truth—nothing was going on between them.

But all the same, Jessica didn't like the look in Eric's eyes as he pressed her twin's hand. Eric was dangerous, that much was clear. And Jessica was going to make sure he had absolutely nothing to do with her sister.

Ten

Elizabeth woke up Saturday morning feeling so confused that she almost didn't remember where she was or what day it was. All night long she had had vague, upsetting dreams about trying to call Jeffrey at camp and getting Eric instead.

During the course of the past few days, since she had learned that Darcy was wrong about the poem, Elizabeth felt more confused than ever about her friendship with Eric. The extent of her own hurt when she believed he was interested in Darcy had upset her deeply. Elizabeth had never really been in this kind of situation before.

And Eric still had no idea Jeffrey even existed. She had planned to mention his name so many times now that it was ridiculous. She was just going to say casually, "Yes, Jeffrey and I . . ." or "You know, Jeffrey always says . . ." Then Eric would ask, reasonably enough, who Jeffrey was, and she would just explain. It would be simple!

The problem was that the golden opportunity Elizabeth was waiting for just hadn't come up. What happened instead was that Darcy had made her jealous, and Elizabeth childishly avoided Eric for two whole days. By the time the misunderstanding had been cleared up, it was pretty clear that Eric thought she liked him. A lot. Why else would she get so enraged at the thought of his writing a poem for someone else?

So now it seemed a little crazy just to "mention" that she had a serious boyfriend working as a camp counselor. Elizabeth had a real problem on her hands.

Not that anything had happened yet between Eric and her. Neither of them had said anything about their feelings, and they hadn't so much as held hands. But the tension between them was so strong that Elizabeth could barely stand it. Every time Eric looked at her she blushed, imagining what it would feel like if he took her in his arms. When he spoke, she found herself staring at his lips, imagining what it would be like to kiss him. And she knew the very next time they were alone together he would kiss her. At the barbecue the night before, she could think about nothing else. She just hoped no one had noticed how strange she was acting.

Elizabeth knew she had some pretty difficult decisions to face. First, she had to tell Eric about Jeffrey before their relationship went one step further. It wasn't fair to Eric—or to Jeffrey.

And then she had to face up to what these new feelings for Eric meant in terms of Jeffrey and her. They had never come right out and promised each other that they wouldn't date other people during the summer, but Elizabeth knew that that had been their understanding. Jeffrey had been writing and calling faithfully, and if he learned she liked another guy, he would be devastated.

Elizabeth was going to have to talk to both of them—and fast.

Jessica was anxious to get over to Darcy's house on Saturday morning. She wanted to tell Darcy about Eric's behavior at the barbecue. But people kept calling—first Lila, long-distance; then Amy Sutton, wanting to have a heart-to-heart talk. Then it turned out that Elizabeth needed the car, and Jessica had no choice but to jump on her bike and pedal over to the Kaymans' house. It seemed like ages before she finally got to Darcy's. She left her bicycle outside and rang the door bell.

"Hi," Darcy said, coming to the door right away. "Jess, I'm so glad you're here! I'm dying to find out what happened last night." She looked around to make sure her mother was out of earshot. "Hurry up! Let's go up to my room," she hissed. "I've *got* to tell you what Sue said last night."

Jessica raced up the stairs to Darcy's bedroom. Darcy shut the door and put her finger to her lips. "Shhh," she warned. "We have to make sure my mom isn't up here."

Jessica listened patiently while Darcy tried to make out her mother's footsteps. "It's OK," Darcy said at last. "I don't want my mom to know we've been messing around with something as dangerous as this."

Jessica sat down on the edge of Darcy's bed. "What's going on? What did Sue say?"

"You tell me first what happened last night," Darcy commanded. "Did you notice anything strange about Eric and his father? How was his dad acting? Did they seem at all nervous or weird to you?"

"Well," Jessica said, "Eric's father *did* seem a

little jumpy. But I thought that was just because Mr. Beckwith, our neighbor, kept insisting he knew him from somewhere. Mr. Beckwith's nice enough, but once he gets on a subject he just won't quit. I got the impression it was bugging Mr. Hankman, so he and Eric left early."

"See? So he acted nervous when he was questioned about his identity. This is straight out of an Agatha Christie book," Darcy declared. "Jess, it's obvious. The Hankmans are trying to hide something!"

"Well, the scariest part of all was Eric," Jessica admitted. "He *really* seemed nervous." She told Darcy all about Eric spilling the iced tea, and Darcy looked triumphant.

"I told you! They're trying to hide the fact that they moved here to protect Eric's real identity. The fact that he isn't Eric Hankman at all, but Christopher Wyeth."

"Christopher Wyeth?" Jessica repeated blankly. "Who's he?"

"According to Sue," Darcy said, dropping her voice and looking intently at Jessica, "he's the suspect in the Ohio murders. Seventeen years old, dark-haired, sensitive and intelligent looking. And he's from Shaker Heights, Ohio," Darcy exclaimed. "Only he isn't in Ohio anymore. He disappeared, and the police have no idea where he is."

Jessica felt a chill run up her spine. "Darcy, you're serious about this, aren't you? You really think Eric could be Chris Wyeth?"

"Well, I'll tell you one thing. I don't think it's worth sitting around and waiting to find out. Jess, we've got to do something fast to find out all we can about this guy."

Jessica thought for a moment. "What about telling someone what we suspect? Don't you think we should talk to our parents about it—or the police? If Eric really is Chris Wyeth, we could be getting ourselves into terrible trouble!"

"No way," Darcy said grimly. "We're not going to mess this up by going to the police before we have some real evidence. No, the thing to do is to make everything seem normal. Perfectly normal. Don't say a word to anyone until we're sure."

"I don't like it," Jessica said, shuddering. "If there really is something dangerous about Eric, I don't like the thought of letting him hang around here. He could meet some girl, start to like her, and then . . ."

Darcy shook her head firmly. "I have every intention of solving this mystery alone," she said. "You and I will be heroes. And Andy Sullivan will finally notice me—really notice me." She tossed back her hair. "Come on, Jess, think about it. The point is, if we're going to find out anything, we've got to use the one advantage we have. Right now you and I are the only ones who know that there may be a connection between Chris Wyeth and Eric Hankman. That means we can really get an edge on the case. Trust me. You can't say *one* word to anybody until we know more."

Jessica nodded earnestly. "OK," she said. "But we have to keep our eyes open, too. If we ever even suspect Eric is going out with some girl here in Sweet Valley, we have to tell the police right away. Is that a promise?"

Darcy nodded. "Promise."

Jessica sighed. "All right. I won't say a word. But what's the plan? How are we supposed to find out more about Eric or Chris or whoever he is?"

"Listen to me," Darcy said, her eyes shining. "The first thing to do is to get hold of Eric's notebook. He writes poems in it, but he also uses it as a diary. I've seen him scribbling in it at work. Jess, you've got to go over to the Hankmans' house today and get that notebook!"

"How?" Jessica demanded. "Why in the world would he give it to me?"

Darcy shrugged. "I don't know. Use your imagination." She thought for a minute, then snapped her fingers. "I've got it! Just pretend you're Liz. Say you want to read some of his poems. Liz is a writer, too. Isn't that something she might do? I don't know, whatever you think will work. Just get your hands on that notebook and bring it back here so we can have a good, close look at it!"

Jessica took a deep breath before pushing the Hankmans' door bell. She hoped this was going to work.

Jessica had assembled an outfit from her sister's wardrobe that looked right for a Saturday afternoon: tan chinos, a cotton polo shirt, and a cotton sweater tied loosely around her neck. She'd had to sneak all the stuff out of the house in a plastic bag, take it back to Darcy's, and change there. She had tied her hair back in a ponytail, rubbed off the last vestiges of makeup, and used Darcy's nail polish remover to take off the polish she had spent hours putting on two days ago.

"You look exactly like her!" Darcy exclaimed. "That's perfect!"

"Wait," Jessica said, frowning. "Can I borrow your wristwatch?"

"Sure." Darcy handed her her watch, and Jessica fastened it on.

"OK," she said. "Here goes nothing."

Now she was standing on the front porch of

the Hankmans' house, waiting for Eric to come to the door. It seemed like ages before he appeared, but Jessica was certain it was only because she was so nervous. The last thing in the world she wanted was to see Eric again—or Chris Wyeth, or whoever he was supposed to be. She sure hoped Darcy knew what she was doing!

At last Eric opened the door. "Liz!" he said, smiling broadly. "Come in!"

Jessica fiddled with her ponytail. "I hope you don't mind me coming over without calling first. I was riding my bike over to Enid's, and I just started thinking about you." She tried to look serious. "I've been thinking a lot about your writing and was wondering if I could take a look at some of your work."

Eric invited her inside. "Why do you sound so formal? Don't you know how glad I am to see you?"

Jessica bit her lip. "Yes—well, uh—" Why was he so glad to see her? She felt her stomach turn over with fear. All she wanted was to get hold of the notebook and get out.

"Eric, I've been thinking more and more about your poetry," she said in her most earnest voice. "I really feel like I can learn a lot about writing from you. Do you think there's any way I could borrow your notebook this afternoon to read some of the poems you've written lately?"

Eric looked puzzled. "Are you mad at me for some reason? Is it because of last night? Look, you can read my poetry any time you want. But why do you sound so—you know—so stiff?"

Jessica stared at him. Exactly how well did her sister know this guy? "I'm sorry," she said shakily. "I'm actually not feeling well. I thought —you know, if I could spend the day reading your poetry . . ." She looked longingly at the door. She was doing a terrible job. Darcy was going to kill her. Her palms were sweating, and she wiped them on her chinos.

"Here," Eric said, handing her the notebook. He gave her a tender, meaningful smile. "Do you feel well enough to get together tonight? Do you still want to meet at the same place?"

Meeting? At the same place? Jessica was horrified. "Uh, yes, yes, of course," Jessica murmured, clutching the notebook to her and jumping nervously to her feet. "I wish I didn't have to stop off at Enid's house," she said, trying to sound sorry to leave, when in fact she could barely wait to get out the door. "But I promised her." She edged toward the front hallway.

"Liz, are you all right? You seem so nervous," Eric said, looking concerned.

Jessica gripped the notebook tightly. "Me? I'm not nervous," she gasped. She could feel her heart pounding. "See you, uh, see you tonight," she said hastily. And with that she escaped, the notebook clutched tightly in her hands.

The notebook was the last thing on her mind once she got safely outside. Elizabeth—meeting Eric! But where? And why had Elizabeth lied to her? The thought of her sister meeting Eric—or Chris—somewhere alone, *at night* . . . Jessica was absolutely horrified.

She would have to do something to stop her twin. But what? And how could she tell Elizabeth that she knew about her date without admitting what she had just done?

Jessica was in such a state of panic that it was several minutes before she even looked at the precious notebook. It didn't appear very incriminating to her. It was just a plain blue spiral notebook with Eric's name and address written in ink on the inside cover. Most of the pages in back were empty. The front section was filled with poems and fragments of poems. Jessica didn't see what Darcy hoped to figure out from this. What had she been expecting—a signed oath in which Eric declared that he was really Chris Wyeth, a murderer, and not just an ordinary seventeen-year-old who happened to like to write poetry? Jessica shuddered. They had much more serious worries now than the notebook. They had to worry about Elizabeth.

Swallowing hard, Jessica set the notebook in the basket of her bike and rode off toward Darcy's, her mind racing. She didn't know what to think. She didn't know if it was smarter to stay quiet about what they suspected or to follow through on their promise and go straight to the police. Eric *was* interested in a girl in Sweet Valley, and it was her very own twin, Elizabeth!

Somehow Jessica had to warn her sister. She had to make sure that whatever Elizabeth did, she wouldn't meet Eric that night—or ever!

Jessica stopped at the corner and balanced herself with one foot on the curb. She noticed that a black Mercedes had turned down the street behind her. It seemed to be moving very slowly. Looking both ways, she turned right, staying close to the curb. The street was deserted except for the Mercedes. It was strange that it was moving so slowly—slowly enough so that the driver was keeping perfect pace with Jessica on her bike. She could see a young man in the front seat who seemed to be staring at her. His window was rolled down, but she couldn't get a very good look at his face.

Her heart began to pound. Speeding up, she

crossed the street in front of the car and took a sudden left.

The car turned left right behind her.

Jessica's mouth was dry as cotton. She sped forward as fast as she could to the next intersection and through the red light, craning her neck behind to see what the car would do. To her dismay the driver, after checking in both directions, followed her through the red light. Jessica speeded up, cycling as hard as she could, and the car speeded up, too.

"Make it stop, make it go away," she moaned. But the black Mercedes was right beside her now. She was really beginning to panic, her heart pounding as her gaze flew involuntarily to her side to track the car's progress. Less than a block from Darcy's house the car passed her, slowed, and a young man jumped out of the passenger side. Jessica was too terrified to really look at him. All she registered was that he was dressed well. She caught a whiff of strong men's cologne and tobacco smoke.

The man stepped right in the path of her bicycle. Too close to avoid him, Jessica quickly applied the brakes. To her surprise, the man put his hands on her handlebars. Jessica's eyes were wide with terror.

"Let go," she said, her voice trembling.

The man gave her bicycle a violent shake.

"Listen to me," he said in a low voice. "If you know what's good for you, you'll stop seeing that boyfriend of yours. You hear me?" Trembling violently, Jessica covered her face with her hands.

"Leave me alone," she cried.

The man gave her bicycle one strong push, knocking it over. Jessica crashed to the ground, hands first to break her fall. She cried out in pain, looking up just in time to see the man snatch the blue notebook.

"Hey!" she cried, jumping to her feet. "Give that back!"

But it was too late. The man had raced off after the Mercedes, grabbed hold of the door, and jumped in. With a squeal the car zoomed off, leaving Jessica huddled next to her bike, shaking uncontrollably. What did he mean when he called Eric her "boyfriend"? And who were the two men?

Still shuddering, Jessica clambered to her feet and gingerly picked up her bicycle. She wasn't hurt, except for her stinging palms. She was just badly shaken. Her bicycle wasn't damaged.

But the notebook was gone.

"He wanted it," Jessica murmured, her eyes wide with fear. "That must be why he stopped me—to get Eric's notebook."

What was there in that notebook, Jessica wondered, that they—whoever *they* were—wanted so badly?

"Wow," Darcy said, shaking her head. "This is a real mess, Jessica. They must be tied in to the murder somehow."

"So what was in that notebook?" Jessica demanded. "I told you, Darcy. I looked through it, and all I saw were poems. I can't figure it out. Why would someone want to knock me off my bicycle just to steal a notebook full of poems?"

"Who knows?" Darcy was pacing back and forth in her bedroom while Jessica, still shaken but somewhat calmer now, changed back into her normal clothing. "Maybe the poems are some kind of code. Or maybe that man was a detective and he wanted something with Eric's fingerprints on it. You know how they sometimes get carried away. Remember, we're not sure what we're dealing with here, Jess. We have to be prepared to accept anything."

Jessica shuddered. "I want to stay out of it. Completely out of it. All I want is to warn Elizabeth not to have anything to do with Eric."

"You're right," Darcy said solemnly. "You should go straight home and tell her that whatever she does, she shouldn't meet him alone.

Not tonight and not ever. You can even tell her I forgive her for trying to steal Eric away from me."

"I still think we should tell someone," Jessica said. "This is getting really serious, Darcy. You didn't see that man's face. He terrified me! They obviously think I'm linked to Eric—or that Liz is. Don't you see that we're both in danger now?"

Darcy nodded. "The thing is, we don't have enough evidence to go to the police. It's all conjecture right now, Jess. What can we say? That Eric seems nervous? That he's from Ohio? We need to have more to go on."

"We could tell someone about what just happened to me," Jessica cried. "Darcy, a man just followed me and knocked me off my bike! Something frightening is going on around here, and I think we need to get help!"

"Just give me the weekend," Darcy begged. "I promise after the weekend we can go to the police. But I just want a little more time. Let me call Sue again. And let's try to figure out a way to find out more about Eric ourselves before we call the police."

Jessica stuffed Elizabeth's clothing back into her bag. "OK," she said. "I don't really care about that. The most important thing is warning Liz." She hurried out of Darcy's bedroom.

"Where are you going?" Darcy cried.

"Home," Jessica said grimly. "I've got to get to Liz right away."

Darcy stared at her. "What are you going to tell her?"

"The truth! Or at least as much of the truth as we think we know," Jessica told her. She hurried down the stairs, raced outside to her bicycle, and stuffed the plastic bag full of clothes into the basket.

One thing was certain. Eric's behavior—combined with what the man in the Mercedes had said about Eric being her "boyfriend"—had proven to Jessica that Elizabeth hadn't been telling the truth.

Something was obviously going on between Elizabeth and Eric. Right now Jessica only cared about one thing—and that was insuring that her sister keep away from him.

Eleven

Jessica barely greeted her mother as she flew into the house. "Where's Liz?" she demanded, trying to keep the urgency out of her voice so she wouldn't make her mother suspicious.

Mrs. Wakefield laughed. "That's what I call a friendly hello to your doting mother," she teased.

Jessica was impatient. "Mom, I need to talk to her," she said. "Is she upstairs?"

Mrs. Wakefield was in the middle of making a cake, and her attention was clearly focused more on mixing the batter than on Jessica's query. "Mmmm," she said, tasting a spoonful of batter. "Honey, Liz has gone off with Enid somewhere. I think they said something about the beach. Not *our* beach but someplace else." She shrugged. "I honestly don't remember. Why?" she added curiously. "Is something up?"

Jessica fidgeted. "When will she be back?" she asked anxiously.

"Not until tomorrow," Mrs. Wakefield said, inspecting the batter's texture. "Actually, to tell the truth, Liz has seemed a little down to me lately," she added. "Haven't you noticed it? I suggested she call Enid this morning. I thought it would be good for her to see friends. She's spent so much time working. And with Jeffrey all the way up north at camp—"

"Not till tomorrow?" Jessica repeated, horrified.

Mrs. Wakefield nodded serenely. "It turns out that Enid really wanted some company this weekend. Her mother had to fly off for a business conference in New Mexico, and Enid was going to be all alone. So Elizabeth packed a bag and headed over to spend the weekend there." She set the spoon down and stared at Jessica. "Honey, what's the matter? You look like you've seen a ghost!"

"Uh, nothing," Jessica muttered. She could almost feel the color draining from her face. If Elizabeth was out with Enid somewhere, if she really planned to spend the weekend there, how was Jessica going to be able to warn her about Eric?

She had to think of some way to keep Elizabeth from going ahead with whatever they had planned for that night. "Will you excuse me?" she mumbled to her mother, ignoring the concerned expression on Mrs. Wakefield's face. Racing upstairs, Jessica dashed for the phone and dialed the Rollinses' phone number.

The phone rang twelve times before Jessica hung up in despair. It figured that the Rollinses didn't have an answering machine!

How on earth was she going to track Elizabeth down before she headed off to meet Eric—or Chris Wyeth, or whoever he was?

Jessica sank down on her bed, her eyes wide with anxiety. All the things she knew about Chris Wyeth kept coming back to her. His irascibility. His sudden mood changes. What the psychologist had predicted about the possibility of him striking again—*soon.*

"Elizabeth!" Jessica moaned softly. She had to think of some way to get a message to her sister. Elizabeth could be in serious danger. And Jessica had to think of some way of protecting her.

Jessica was in no mood to hang out at the Dairi Burger with Darcy and several friends from Sweet Valley High. It was late Saturday afternoon, and she and Darcy had been running all over town, trying to find Enid and Elizabeth. Of course, they had run into lots of Jessica's friends, and a quarter of an hour earlier Amy Sutton had insisted on their coming along for a quick milk shake.

Jessica was tired and upset. The last measure was to stop by the Rollinses' house and leave Elizabeth a note, but she hadn't been crazy about the idea. What if Elizabeth missed the note somehow and went off anyway to meet Eric?

Despite herself, she had gotten dragged into the crowded, popular hamburger place. Now she was wedged into a booth with Darcy, Amy, and two old friends from school, Aaron Dallas and Winston Egbert. Amy introduced Darcy to the two boys, and at once Darcy was busy trying to charm them. But Jessica didn't feel like taking part in the cheerful conversation as everyone tried to catch up on one another's summer activities. She was too worried about her sister.

"Hey," Darcy said under her breath to Jessica. "Look who's here!"

Jessica shot a glance toward the counter. Eric Hankman was holding a tray and glancing around. Jessica's stomach fell.

Amy's eyes widened. "Who is he? He's really cute!"

Darcy gave her a reproachful look. "I thought so, too—at first," she said forebodingly. Before Darcy could say another word, Eric caught sight of her and came over to say hello.

Aaron and Winston were deep in discussion about soccer and had to be interrupted for introductions. Eric, who had just bought a burger, seemed to be in a good mood.

"Can I join you?" he asked, pulling up a chair.

Jessica and Darcy exchanged nervous glances, but there wasn't any way to stop him.

"Forget it!" Aaron cried to Winston. "With Jeffrey on the team, we've got every chance in the world of being All-State this coming fall!"

Jessica cringed. The look Darcy gave her showed that the redhead had the same thought she did. How much, if anything, did Eric know about Elizabeth and Jeffrey?

Jessica suddenly jumped into the conversation, eager to do her best to keep it away from soccer—and Jeffrey French. "Has anyone seen that new James Bond movie?" she asked.

"I have," Eric said, smiling. He pulled a chair up to the end of the booth. Meanwhile, the two boys were still intent on discussing sports.

"Listen, Jeffrey's good, but he isn't that good," Winston continued. There didn't seem to be any way to stop them. Jessica felt ready to scream, she was so frustrated and anxious.

"We shouldn't be talking this way in front of Jess," Aaron said affectionately, leaning over to ruffle her hair. "You'll go home and tell Liz, right? And we know how loyal Liz is. One bad thing said about Jeffrey and she'll hate us all for months!"

Dead silence followed as Eric suddenly seemed to pay attention to what was being said. "Who is Jeffrey?" he asked almost casually.

Winston, famous for being a clown, pretended to be horrified. "What? You mean you know the Wakefield twins and don't know about Jeffrey French? He's the light of Elizabeth's life. Or—as you common mortals put it—her boyfriend."

"And an ace soccer player," Aaron added.

Eric's expression changed swiftly, as if a storm had blown up in a clear summer sky. He set his hamburger down and cleared his throat with effort. "Where is he now?" he asked. He was remarkably controlled, Jessica thought. But she could see a muscle twitching in his jaw.

"He's a camp counselor for the summer up north," Aaron said. "But you'll meet him when he gets back. He's a great guy. I bet you'll really like him."

"Sure," Eric said abruptly, pushing back his chair and getting to his feet. The look on his face was positively terrifying. Jessica's heart began to pound.

"Eric, where are you going?" she demanded.

Eric didn't answer. He spun on his heel and stormed out of the Dairi Burger, his face angry and his fists clenched.

Jessica looked at Darcy with an agonized and helpless expression. This was all they needed to turn an emergency into total disaster.

It was bad enough before. Now Eric had a reason to be furious with Elizabeth. And God only knew what Eric Hankman would do once his affection had turned to fury.

Elizabeth stared at her watch. There was no denying it—she'd been stood up. She was supposed to meet Eric in front of the Beach Disco at eight o'clock, and it was ten minutes to nine. If it had been anyone else, she would have stuck around for a while, thinking he might be late. But she knew Eric was always early for everything.

She had already called the Hankmans' house from the Beach Disco, and there was no answer. The question was, where was Eric? And why in the world hadn't he met her there tonight?

Elizabeth's disappointment was sharpened by the fact that she had been looking forward to her date with Eric all day long. She and Enid had spent a nice calm afternoon together. They had driven out to a special beach Enid loved, almost an hour away from Sweet Valley. Being with her best friend had really helped Elizabeth understand how confused and distressed she had been lately. And talking through her feelings with Enid made her realize that her emotions were too strong to dispense with easily. She really cared for Eric a great deal. Her ambivalence seemed to have faded into the background as the hour they were supposed to meet got closer. Finally, all she could think about was how excited she was. She had spent ages getting ready at Enid's house, and by the time she left, she was really looking forward to their date. The dawning realization that he wasn't going to show up made her heart sink. She had no idea what could have gone wrong.

Sighing, Elizabeth got into the Fiat and drove slowly through the dusky streets. She didn't really want to go back to Enid's house yet. She felt incredibly let down, and the thought of being with her best friend right now didn't appeal to her. She decided to take a drive before returning to the Rollinses' house.

After a few minutes on the coast road, Elizabeth frowned into her rearview mirror. Was it her imagination, or was that car following her? In the twilight it was hard to make out the type of car or the face of the driver, but she felt fairly certain it had been behind her since she'd left the Beach Disco.

Elizabeth accelerated, taking a sharp right at the next intersection. The other car followed.

She swallowed hard, then took a very sharp left. The Fiat's tires squealed as she rounded the corner, but the other car stayed behind her. Elizabeth was beginning to panic. She locked her car door, took a deep breath, and pulled off the road. The car following her, which she could now see was a deep blue sedan, pulled up next to the Fiat, and the driver rolled down his window.

"Miss, could I speak with you?" a middle-aged man with a mustache asked. He was attractively dressed, wearing a dark suit, and seemed very crisp and professional. Then he flashed something at her in a gesture she'd seen only in movies. He was showing her an FBI identification card.

Elizabeth wasn't nervous, just surprised. Why would an FBI agent want to talk to her? The sedan parked behind her, and the man, still looking very efficient, got out of the car and walked toward her.

"My name is Riordon," he told her. "I wonder if you could answer a few questions for me. Do you know a young man named Eric Hankman?"

Elizabeth was surprised. "Why, yes, I do, as a matter of fact. I was supposed to meet him tonight, but he—" She broke off, blushing.

The man nodded expressionlessly. "Didn't meet you," he murmured, writing something down. "How would you describe this young man? Anything unusual about him? Any reason you feel suspicious when you're with him?"

"No," Elizabeth said, frowning. "No, none at all." She cleared her throat. "Why? Can I ask you why you're asking me these questions?" How had the agent found her, she wondered. How had he known she was a friend of Eric's? Was it possible he'd been following her—following both of them—for a while?

The agent was quiet. "We can't really say at this point, miss. We're trying to ascertain certain facts about Eric." He cleared his throat. "No idea where Eric could be found tonight, then?"

Elizabeth shook her head, more confused than ever.

"Well, thank you very much," the man said, closing his notebook.

Elizabeth watched him get back into the blue sedan. Something peculiar was going on. But what? Where was Eric? And why in the world were there FBI agents trying to find out more about him?

*　*　*

"Why would an FBI agent want to follow Eric?" Enid asked sensibly. She had listened to Elizabeth's story with her usual calm attentiveness, and now seemed to be mulling through the details. The girls were sitting together in the Rollinses' living room, drinking cocoa and talking about what had taken place that evening.

"Good question. I have no idea. But then, to be honest, I don't really know all that much about Eric." Elizabeth frowned. "I know he's from Ohio. I know his parents recently separated and that he's got some pretty sad memories he's had to deal with. Otherwise—I don't know, he's pretty defensive about his past. He doesn't seem to like to talk about it."

"Well, if he has painful memories, it makes sense he wouldn't want to dwell on the past. But that doesn't explain why the FBI would be looking for him." Enid frowned and shook her head. "It's weird, I have to admit. But it seems to me that there are two completely separate issues here, Liz. The first and most important one is how you feel about Eric. I think you've got to straighten out how you're feeling about Jeffrey and then be brutally honest with yourself about what you want from this guy. The next stage is to talk to Eric openly and find out what he wants. Like why he stood you up

160

tonight. Who knows? He may be afraid of what he's feeling for you. Maybe he even found out about Jeffrey somehow."

Elizabeth looked distraught. "I hope not! But you're right, Enid. I've got some serious thinking to do."

"And then," Enid continued warmly, "once you know how you feel and what you want, you've got to ask Eric if he can think of any reason why someone would be following him."

Elizabeth nodded. She knew Enid was right. Now the only thing to do was to find Eric. They needed to talk, and the sooner she found him the better.

Suddenly Enid clapped her hand over her mouth. "I can't believe it," she gasped. "Liz, you're going to kill me. I have a note to give you, and I forgot all about it till right now!"

"A note?" Elizabeth repeated blankly.

Enid nodded. "I found it under the door when I got back from the grocery store this evening. You had already gone out. It must've gotten slipped under the mat instead of the door, so it was hidden. Anyway, it's from Jessica, not from Eric. She wrote her name on the outside. But" —Enid sighed—"you're not going to believe it. Muffy must've gotten to it or something because look, it's all torn up. You can't even read it." Muffy was the Rollinses' playful cat, famous for exactly this kind of domestic damage.

Elizabeth stared down at the illegible, torn-up shreds that used to be a note from her sister. "Oh, well," she said philosophically. "Whatever it is, I'm sure it can wait." Right then Elizabeth was too worried about Eric to think about Jessica. She paced back and forth in the living room. "I'm going to keep trying to reach Eric. Sooner or later he's got to go home. Right?"

Enid looked thoughtfully at her friend. "Liz," she said after a moment. "I have an idea. Why don't we get in my car first thing tomorrow morning and drive up to my aunt's cabin in the mountains? You look exhausted to me. I think you really need to get away and think through some of the stuff you're feeling."

Elizabeth looked upset. "What about Eric? I need to call him and find out why he didn't show up tonight!"

Enid shrugged. "Let it wait till Monday. I think you could use the peace and quiet."

Elizabeth smiled. "You're a really good friend," she said. "It sure would be nice to be far away from all of this. Let's do it, Enid. Let's just take off first thing!"

"Good. I'm glad that's settled," Enid said firmly. "Meanwhile, I think we could both use a good night's sleep."

Elizabeth nodded. But she couldn't put the image of the FBI agent out of her mind. Why on earth was he following Eric?

*   *   *

Jessica paced back and forth in Darcy's bedroom, her face pale and her eyes frantic with worry. "I don't see how you can eat," she moaned, watching Darcy working her way through a bag of peanut M&M's. Darcy, who had come down with a cold overnight, was still in her pajamas—and busily trying to eat everything she could find to restore her strength. "Don't you realize my sister could be in terrible danger even as we speak?"

"She isn't in terrible danger, silly. She's up in the mountains with Enid," Darcy pointed out. "Which means that nothing happened to her last night, right?" She stopped to blow her nose. "Sorry," she said hoarsely. "I'm really stuffed up."

Jessica had been absolutely terrified the night before until Elizabeth called home to tell her parents that she and Enid were going to drive up to the mountains Sunday morning and wouldn't be back until dinnertime or later. Then, and only then, had Jessica calmed down slightly. But she was still extremely anxious on her sister's behalf. Not until she was able to talk to Elizabeth in person would Jessica really feel better.

Darcy seemed to be relishing the mystery without getting panicky. Since she had caught a cold, her attention was largely taken up with her own health—she kept taking her temperature, making cups of tea, and eating—claiming it was best to "feed a cold." "Look, Jess," she said, sniffling. "Everything's under control. As long as you don't panic, I don't see what can go wrong."

"I want to tell my parents—or the police," Jessica said. "Darcy, we promised. The deal was that we would keep it just between us until Eric started to date a girl in Sweet Valley. That's already happened! And it just turns out to be my sister. My *only* sister," she added pointedly. "One whom I happen to hope to keep. So I say we call the police—right now."

Darcy sneezed. "Just wait till tomorrow," she begged. "I talked to Sue right before you came over. She said she express-mailed a copy of the police composite that ran in the papers. She sent it yesterday, so it'll be here tomorrow." Darcy blew her nose again. "I'm going to stay home from work anyway, so I'll be here when the mail comes." She looked pointedly at Jessica. "By tomorrow we'll have good, solid evidence to go on. Either Eric looks like the composite or he doesn't."

"But what about Liz?" Jessica wailed. "What about the chances of her getting hurt before the composite gets here?"

"I told you, Jess. The situation is totally under control. Your sister is safe, up in the mountains with Enid. What can possibly happen?
She'll go to work tomorrow. If she sees Eric at
all, it will just be to say hello in the coffee shop.
Nothing can happen," Darcy promised. "Not
before we get a chance to study the composite.
And I swear to you—if Eric turns out to look
close enough, we'll call the police—right away."
She shuddered. "I'm scared enough of him already. One more bit of proof and wild horses
couldn't keep me from calling the police!"

Jessica twisted a lock of hair between her
fingers. She was dreading going to work the
next morning, but she was determined not to
let her sister out of her sight. No way was she
going to let Elizabeth spend one second alone
with Eric or Chris or whoever he was. Elizabeth's life might depend on it!

Darcy woke up Monday morning feeling unusually nervous. She still felt lousy from her
cold, but more than that, she had an apprehensive feeling, as if something awful were about
to happen. She called Dan Weeks to explain
that she was sick and wouldn't be able to come
into work. She thought about asking Dan to
keep an eye on Elizabeth, but she knew that

would be ridiculous—and that Dan would want to know why.

"Is Elizabeth in yet?" she asked instead. It was nine o'clock, and she knew Elizabeth was likely to come in early on Mondays to get a head start on the week ahead.

"She was in about half an hour ago. But then Seth asked her if she could spend the whole day with him out on special assignment, in Los Palmos. I don't think she'll be in the office all day."

"Oh," Darcy said. She felt relieved. That meant that Elizabeth would be far away from Eric, at any rate—at least until after she'd had a chance to look at the composite Sue was sending.

Nonetheless, the apprehensive feeling didn't go away. As the morning wore on, it got stronger and stronger.

At ten-thirty the front door bell rang, and Darcy rushed downstairs, still wearing her pajamas. It was the express mail package from Ohio.

"Darcy Kaymen?" the mailman asked her.

Darcy nodded. Her fingers were trembling as she took the envelope from him. She was so anxious to see the composite that she barely noticed the note Sue had included. Her heart started to pound, and her mouth went dry as she stared down at the photocopy of the sketch the police artist had drawn from witnesses' descriptions.

The resemblance was uncanny. The dark, curly hair, the strong jaw, the wide-set, slightly mysterious eyes. Darcy's hand shook as she held the composite up for a better look.

There was no denying it. This drawing looked a lot like Eric Hankman.

Darcy raced upstairs. She had to change into her clothes and get to the office as fast as possible. She had to tell Jessica about this—and somehow they had to get hold of Elizabeth. Darcy knew they couldn't risk it any longer. They had to warn Elizabeth, and then they had to go to the police and tell them that they thought they'd found Chris Wyeth.

"But she isn't here!" Jessica cried, her blue-green eyes wide with horror.

"I know, I know," Darcy cried. The girls were in the library with the door closed. Darcy was so worked up, she was trembling. And Jessica was beginning to shake, too.

"You mean Eric really *is* Chris Wyeth? He's really a murderer?" Jessica's face was as white as paper.

"It sure looks like it," Darcy said in a low, frightened voice. She handed Jessica the composite.

Jessica groaned. "Darcy, I told you we should've called the police before! What if Liz runs into Eric somehow before we can get to her and warn her who he really is?" Her eyes flashed with terror. "Remember, he's got a reason to be mad at her now. He knows about Jeffrey."

Darcy shook her head, her eyes dark with fear. "We just can't let that happen, Jess. Whatever we do, we've got to find her before Eric does."

Jessica stared helplessly at Darcy. She couldn't believe how frightened she was. She just hoped Elizabeth was still with Seth, and wherever they were, that they were far away from Eric.

Twelve

"Is anything wrong, Liz?" Seth asked Elizabeth. "That must be the third time I've asked you for something when you haven't heard me."

Elizabeth reddened. "Sorry, Seth," she mumbled. "I guess I'm a little bit tired from the weekend, that's all. I promise I'll pay attention from now on."

To show him she meant business, Elizabeth took her notebook out of her bag and furiously began making notes in it about the last interview Seth had conducted. They were out in Los Palmos interviewing teachers about the possibility of a strike in the late summer, and Elizabeth knew how important it was to act as backup to Seth and keep careful notes in case he missed something.

But she just couldn't keep her mind on anything. All she could think about was Eric.

"Look," Seth said, glancing at his watch, "it's almost four o'clock already. We've put in a good long day, and we're not getting anything more done out here anyway. Why don't you let me drop you off at home? We can write this up tomorrow when we're both fresh."

Elizabeth shook her head. "No. Let me try to write it up myself, Seth. I know I've been next to useless today. Why don't you drop me off at the office? I'll write up our notes, get some kind of rough draft together, and you can get to work on it first thing in the morning."

Seth looked doubtful. "Well, if you're sure," he said. "But we won't even get back to the office till five o'clock. You really think you'll feel like working then?"

Elizabeth nodded intently. "I really want to," she insisted.

Five o'clock, she was thinking. Just about the time people would be leaving the Western Building. If she was lucky, she'd be able to find Eric and spend a couple of minutes with him alone.

She still hadn't seen him since he stood her up on Saturday night. In fact, she had counted on being able to talk to him today at work, and then the minute she walked through the door Seth had cornered her and asked her to go with him to Los Palmos. Every minute now seemed like agony to Elizabeth as she tried to understand why Eric was avoiding her and how she could convince him how she really felt.

One thing was certain. Elizabeth had faced the fact this weekend that she had very strong feelings for Eric. The time had come for real honesty between them. She wanted to explain to him her predicament about Jeffrey and hoped they could decide, together, what to do. But all that depended on one big unanswered question: did Eric feel the same way Elizabeth did? And if he did, why in the world had he been avoiding her?

On the way home, Seth said, "Look, Liz, you don't have to tell me what's bugging you if you don't want, but I want you to know that I'm here to listen if you need help. OK?"

Elizabeth gave him a grateful smile. "I know I haven't been much use today," she said apologetically. She wished she could confide in Seth, even ask his advice, but she knew it would be inappropriate. Seth was part of her work life, not her personal life. "Thanks for being so understanding," she added.

"Are you sure you want to go back to work?" he asked with concern when they reached the Western Building.

Elizabeth nodded emphatically. She really did want to try to redeem herself by writing up these notes. And she wanted to try to find Eric. In fact, she was thinking so hard about Eric and whether or not she'd be able to find him in the coffee shop that she was completely oblivious to Darcy and Jessica when she got out of Seth's Toyota.

The two girls had been watching for Seth's car from the window of the news office on the fifth floor. The minute they saw Elizabeth get out, they began to wave their arms and cry out her name.

But Elizabeth didn't notice. She marched straight into the office building, her mind on one thing and one thing only: getting Eric Hankman alone to find out how he really felt.

"Eric?" Elizabeth said softly. The coffee shop was deserted, and Eric was sitting at a corner table, fiddling with his pen. His jaw was set, and he was glowering.

His expression darkened when he saw her, and he immediately looked away.

"Eric, what is it? Aren't you even glad to see me?" Elizabeth cried.

Eric stared at the floor, expressionless. "Why should I be?" A muscle jerked in his jaw, and Elizabeth felt a chill run up her spine.

The bell sounded as a customer came in. It was a young woman with a little boy—an adorable child who didn't look older than four or five. Eric excused himself to go wait on them. He poured a cup of coffee for the woman and made a sandwich for the child. Elizabeth watched all this in a state of agony. Finally, Eric was done. The mother and child sat down in front of the window, and the child began to eat his sandwich.

"Eric, we've got to talk. Alone," Elizabeth said desperately. "Come on. These people will be fine for a couple of minutes. I just have to talk to you."

"Why?" Eric cried, his face contorting. "What's the use?"

"Because—" Elizabeth broke off. She couldn't tell him how she felt. Not then. Not when he was so filled with fury.

He searched her face, then grabbed her arm, almost roughly. "Come on," he said. "You want to talk? Then let's talk." He tore off his apron and pulled Elizabeth out of the shop and into the corridor. He was almost running, and Elizabeth's arm hurt where he gripped her so tightly. Elizabeth felt tears of pain fill her eyes. "Eric," she moaned. "You're hurting me!"

"Liz!" Elizabeth heard her twin shriek. Jessica, spotting the two as they left the coffee shop, came charging after them, her face filled with terror.

Elizabeth stared back at her. Something in Jessica's voice made her stop dead in her tracks. "It's my sister," she said to Eric. "She sounds upset. She—"

But Eric's face was set. "Forget her," he said roughly. He broke into a run, pulling her after him. She had to race to keep up with him, but soon they turned into a tiny alley around the corner and fell back against the brick wall, out of breath. Jessica and Darcy tore right past, and Elizabeth could hear her twin crying, "We've got to find her!" Eric clapped his hand over her mouth so she couldn't call out to them, and suddenly, though she knew it was crazy, Elizabeth was frightened.

"Don't," she moaned, trying to pull away from his hand.

Eric just stared at her, his eyes grim. "You're the one who thinks we still have something to talk about," he said tersely. "And one thing's for sure, Liz. If we're going to talk, we're going to talk *alone*."

"Where is she?" Jessica demanded. Her sides were heaving, and she was completely out of breath. "Didn't she run this way?"

"I—I don't know," Darcy gasped. The two had run to the end of the block and were staring around them in wild confusion. No sight of Eric—and no sight of Elizabeth.

Jessica burst into tears. "He's got her," she sobbed. "Darcy, he's got her!" She was trembling all over. "We've got to get help!"

Darcy grabbed her arm. "Let's run back to the office and call the police. Come on!"

Jessica stared after her as Darcy tore back toward the Western Building. She couldn't stand the thought of leaving her sister with that maniacal killer. But where had he taken her? Where was she?

"Liz!" she screamed at the top of her lungs. "L-i-i-z!"

But there was no answer.

Still sobbing, Jessica stumbled after Darcy. The girls raced through the doors into the main corridor just as Mr. Beckwith came racing out, his face ashen.

"Girls, you have to help me!" he cried. "There's a child in the coffee shop who's choking. I tried the Heimlich maneuver and it didn't work. Unless someone does something, he's going to die!"

Thirteen

Jessica stared at the scene inside the coffee shop in horror. The little boy was laid out flat on the floor and was obviously unable to breathe.

Mr. Beckwith, who had been in the coffee shop when the child began to choke, grabbed Jessica by the arm. "I want you to run outside to the pay phone to call an ambulance. And meanwhile, shout for a doctor."

Jessica felt as though her feet were frozen to the ground. She wanted to tell him about Elizabeth, wanted to say that even as they spoke her sister's life was in danger, too. But she couldn't get the words out.

"Go!" Mr. Beckwith cried, giving her a firm

push as he realized that she was too stunned to move.

She stumbled toward the door, her heart pounding. Once outside in the glare of light and traffic, adrenaline caused her to speed up, and she raced for the pay phone. She was just reaching for the receiver when Mr. Hankman stepped out of the Press Club, his raincoat over his arm.

"Why, Jessica!" he exclaimed. "Is everything all right?"

Jessica felt tears spill over. "No," she gasped. She was about to explain when Mr. Beckwith came tearing out of the coffee shop across the street. "Help!" he cried. "Please—someone—get the police, get an ambulance! There's a little boy in the coffee shop choking to death!"

Mr. Hankman stared at Jessica.

"Is that true?" he demanded.

Jessica nodded, still too panic-stricken to speak. The next thing she knew, Mr. Hankman was charging into the building. Jessica raced after him, almost colliding with Eric, who was striding purposefully back into the coffee shop.

"Dad, don't!" Eric cried, grabbing onto his father and trying to stop him.

Jessica couldn't hold back the floodgate of frightened tears. "Where's my sister?" she cried to Eric. "What have you done to my sister?"

Eric looked at her blankly, then back at his father. "Would someone please tell me what is going on here?" he cried.

Mr. Hankman stared at his son, his eyes full of emotion. "A child is in danger in there and I'm going to help him," he said. With that he ran into the coffee shop, with Eric in pursuit, an expression of horror on his face.

Just then Elizabeth rounded the corner, her face pale. "Lizzie!" Jessica shrieked, throwing her arms around her sister. "Oh, Liz, thank heaven you're all right!"

"Why wouldn't I be?" Elizabeth said blankly.

"I've been running up and down this stupid street," Jessica said, gasping as she tried to catch her breath, "just trying to find you. Liz, do you have any idea who Eric Hankman really is?"

Elizabeth stared at her. But neither of them had time to say another word. At just that moment, a blood-piercing scream came from inside the coffee shop. Elizabeth grabbed Jessica's arm and pulled her inside.

"Help him! Somebody help my little boy!" the woman was screaming as the twins crowded into the coffee shop. The child's face was beginning to turn a terrifying shade of purplish-blue.

"He's choking on a big bite of bread," his mother wailed. "Someone help him, please!"

Elizabeth grabbed onto a chair to steady herself. She had never seen a sight as horrifying. "I can't look," she murmured, turning her face away.

"We need a doctor! Help, please!" the little boy's mother shouted as Mr. Hankman pushed his way through to where the child lay writhing.

Mr. Hankman leaned over and felt for his pulse. "Eric," he said in a tense, controlled voice, "I want you to bring me the sharpest knife you've got behind the counter. Bring a plastic straw and a couple of clean dish towels. Then I want you to take this little boy's mother out of here."

Eric flew behind the counter to obey his father.

"What's he doing?" Jessica gasped, horrified.

"He's going to do some sort of operation," Darcy said, watching the proceedings with a mixture of dread and fascination. "I think it's called a tracheotomy. You see, he has to open up the windpipe so the boy can breathe."

Eric had already grabbed a tablecloth and fashioned a makeshift screen to shield the child, but his mother refused to leave him. She knelt by the little boy, holding his head in her lap while Mr. Hankman made an expert incision in the child's neck that allowed air to reach his windpipe below the obstruction. He used the straw to keep the incision open until doctors could replace it with a proper tube in the hospital, and he stopped the flow of blood with the dish towels. "Eric," he said in the same calm voice, "I want you to get on the phone now and call Fowler Memorial. Tell them we've done an emergency tracheotomy and the patient is stable. Tell them to send an ambulance right away." He knelt back, wiping beads of sweat from his forehead.

"Is he all right?" the mother cried fearfully, staring down at her child, whose color was beginning to return to normal.

Mr. Hankman carefully rearranged the towels around the child's neck. Then he patted the woman on the shoulder. The boy's chest was lifting as his lungs filled with air.

Mr. Hankman patted her on the shoulder. "He's fine," he said, getting heavily to his feet. His expression seemed very sad as he met Eric's eyes.

Eric stared down at the ground.

"I don't know how to thank you," the woman said, wiping tears from her eyes. "Please tell me who you are so I can thank you properly, once Timmy has been taken care of in the hospital."

Mr. Beckwith was staring at Mr. Hankman. "I don't believe it," he whispered. "No wonder you look familiar!"

Mr. Hankman lifted his hand in protest. "Please," he said quietly. "For my son's sake . . ."

But Mr. Beckwith was too excited to be silenced. "Do you all know who this is?" he cried triumphantly to the crowd that had gathered in the small coffee shop.

"Come on, Eric," Mr. Hankman cried, grabbing his son's hand.

"Eric!" Elizabeth moaned, watching his father pull him out of the shop. "Eric, let me come with you! Where are you going?"

But the crowd closed in between them. The look on Eric's face was so plaintive and sad that Elizabeth felt as if her heart was breaking.

"That's Dr. Ryan!" Mr. Beckwith announced. "I never would've recognized him till I saw him operate on that child. But that's him. He's the one who testified against Frank DeLucca!"

Jessica and Darcy stared at each other. "You mean—you mean Eric isn't Chris Wyeth?" Darcy muttered weakly. "But the composite . . ."

Elizabeth was staring at Mr. Beckwith. "How do you know?" she demanded. "Mr. Hankman doesn't look one bit like Dr. Ryan. He has dark hair and a beard, and he's much, much heavier. And besides—"

"Well, of course he looks different," Mr. Beckwith said. "That's the whole point of the witness protection program."

Elizabeth felt her chest constricting. She could barely sort out all the things she was feeling. Part of her didn't want to admit that what Mr. Beckwith was saying could be true. But the other part sensed, almost at once, that it must be. No wonder Eric had been so secretive about his past. No wonder he seemed so bitter sometimes.

Her heart went out to them both. Mr. Hankman—Dr. Ryan—had risked exposing them both in order to save this little boy. A true doctor, he couldn't possibly have stood by and watched the child suffocate without trying to help.

But what would happen to the Hankmans now that their identities had been revealed? Elizabeth didn't really want to find out. She was terrified of what it might mean. What if they had to leave Sweet Valley?

"I've got to follow them," she muttered, trying to push her way through the crowd.

She hadn't even had a chance to tell Eric how she felt about him. She was so anxious to tell him about Jeffrey, to try to figure out what to do. She had been on the verge of spilling it all out to him when they had heard the terrified cries from the coffee shop. Eric had charged back in to the shop to help before

Elizabeth had a chance to say a word. And now he was gone.

Jessica and Darcy were too busy arguing about Sue and the composite and all the incriminating evidence against Eric from Shaker Heights to notice Elizabeth leaving. But she had barely left the shop when Jessica, her face turning pale, grabbed Darcy's arm.

The ambulance had just arrived, and two paramedics rushed in with a stretcher to take little Timothy to the hospital. But that wasn't what had caught Jessica's attention. It was the young man in the gray suit who had been standing in the back of the shop the whole time Mr. Hankman was operating on Timothy.

Jessica had just caught sight of him. And what she saw made her stomach flip over. He was following her sister as she hurried off to the garage in search of the Fiat.

"Darcy, forget about Chris Wyeth for now. We've got to get help. I think Liz may be in trouble—and the kind of trouble *I'm* talking about is real!"

The man in the gray suit was the same one who had knocked her off her bicycle and stolen Eric's notebook!

Elizabeth drove over to the Hankmans' house as fast as she could. All she could think about was trying to convince Eric's father that it would be all right to stay in Sweet Valley—even now that his true identity had been revealed.

Mr. Hankman, looking haggard, opened the front door and invited Elizabeth in. The whole house was in disarray. Mr. Hankman had a suitcase open on the coffee table in the living room and was hurling documents into it from his desk. Eric was pacing back and forth. He looked terrible.

"Liz!" he cried when he saw her. He raced over and threw his arms around her, burying his head in her hair. "Is it ever good to see you," he murmured. "I'm so sorry about all this . . . all this lying, all this secretiveness. But it had to be that way."

Elizabeth started to cry. "Is it true?" she demanded, turning to Mr. Hankman.

He nodded ruefully. "I'm afraid it is. And I'm afraid I've consigned my family to endlessly running away." He looked exhausted, and there were tears forming in his eyes. "My wife and daughter were supposed to come out and join us in a few months if all had gone well. Now it doesn't look as if we'll ever be able to make it again as a whole family." He sighed. "I knew when I testified what a big step I was taking. But I don't think I realized the impact it would have on my wife and kids." He looked sadly at Eric. "Just when we got settled here, when Eric started to make a few friends—"

"But why do you have to leave?" Elizabeth cried. "No one will hurt you here. Sweet Valley is different!"

"I wish I could believe that," Mr. Hankman said. He gave Elizabeth a long, thoughtful look. "You're a wonderful girl, Elizabeth. I can tell how brave you are and how much you believe people are good. But suppose I were to tell you that Frank DeLucca has friends all over the country, even right here in Sweet Valley? Friends who would be willing to pay millions of dollars to the one citizen who would tell them where they could find Eric or me?"

Elizabeth suddenly remembered the man in the blue car. "But you have people following you, right? People who are trying to protect you?"

Eric looked grim. "The people following us aren't trying to protect us. They're really De-Lucca's men. My dad thinks that people in town have tipped them off that we've moved here."

Eric's father nodded in agreement. "Much as I like to believe the best of people, I don't want to endanger my son's life any more than I already have." He patted Elizabeth on the shoulder. "I know all this must be hard to understand. It probably sounds like something you'd see on television or something. But I'm afraid it's real. *Very* real. Our only choice is to get out of Sweet Valley as fast as we possibly can."

"But you don't understand Sweet Valley!" Elizabeth cried. "Everyone in the coffee shop thought you were a hero. In fact, what you did was heroic enough in the first place. But the fact that you risked exposing your real identity to save that little boy makes you even more of a hero. If you stay, don't you think people will protect you?"

"I told you, Dad. Liz is an idealist," Eric said. His voice sounded very sad.

"I can see that, Eric." Mr. Hankman looked intently at Elizabeth. "I wish I could believe that. Maybe some people do think I'm a hero. But those people are just an insignificant handful compared to all the apathetic people who would just sit by and watch if anyone tried to hurt us."

"Not here," Elizabeth protested. "Not in Sweet Valley!"

"I think it's easy to be idealistic when you haven't been through what we've been through," Mr. Hankman said tiredly. "I honestly believed that testifying against DeLucca was the right thing. After what I heard from his victim, I couldn't remain quiet and watch DeLucca go free. I just couldn't." Mr. Hankman sank down on the couch, burying his face in his hands. "But I had no idea what it would do to my family." He looked hopelessly at Eric. "I'll never believe in people again," he said at last. "I think most of them are well-meaning enough, but when it comes right down to it, they won't risk their own safety. There were plenty of people around who could have testified against DeLucca. But no one was willing."

"But you were," Elizabeth said in a low, clear voice. "You were the one to prove your own theory wrong. You have to believe there are others like you."

Mr. Hankman didn't acknowledge Elizabeth's comment. "We've got to pack things up here," he said sadly. "I hate to be the one to say this, Eric, but we've got to get out of here right away."

"But what about our contact in the protection program, Dad?" Eric asked. "Shouldn't we get in touch with him? He'll know what to do."

"We're on our own now, Eric, and we're leaving Sweet Valley tonight! There's nothing else we can do. It's too late."

Eric and Elizabeth stared at each other, stricken.

"I know how hard it's going to be to leave," Mr. Hankman added. "And I know you two are going to want to be alone." He picked up his suitcase and headed upstairs. "Just a few minutes, OK?"

Eric cleared his throat as he stared at Elizabeth.

"I can't stand it!" Elizabeth cried. "Eric, you can't leave! You just can't!" She flung herself into his arms, tears streaming down her cheeks. "We've got to think of something. Help me think, Eric. There's got to be some way out of this."

Eric shook his head. There was a dull, pained expression in his eyes. "Liz, I was so afraid this was going to happen. The minute I met you I knew this was too good to be true. There's something about you." He shook his head. "I know it sounds kind of corny, but the minute I met you I felt like it was fate or something. Like you and I could really matter to each other. It's never happened to me like that before."

Elizabeth felt a huge lump forming in her throat. "Eric," she gasped, the tears still spilling over, "I can't bear to let you go! Not now!"

But there was nothing they could do. She could hear Mr. Hankman moving around upstairs, putting things in his suitcase. It seemed inevitable. Eric was going to leave just when she had realized how she felt about him. He was going to take off with his father and change his name and identity, and the Eric Hankman she had fallen in love with would just vanish, like a beautiful mirage.

"There're so many things we never got to say to each other," Eric said softly. "I still don't understand about Jeffrey. You're in love with him, aren't you?"

Elizabeth stared down at the floor. "I could just say no," she said. "Or yes. That would be easier. The truth is, I'm feeling very confused. I *am* in love with Jeffrey. But I also know I've fallen in love with you, too. Do you think it's possible to be in love with two people at once? I don't know what to think any more, Eric. I've never felt like this before."

"Oh, Liz," Eric said, throwing his arms around her and holding her tight, so tight she thought he'd never let go. "Why did I have to meet you now—when everything's so hopelessly messed up?"

"You know," Elizabeth said weakly, wiping her eyes, "I really don't know anything about you. I don't even know your real name."

"It's Michael," he said, leaning over tenderly to wipe the tears from her face. "Michael Ryan. And it isn't true that you don't know anything about me. Under the mask of Eric Hankman I've told you more about myself than I've ever told anyone. I told you how I felt about life and art and poetry. All the things that really matter to me. You've been a wonderful friend, Liz. I'm never going to forget you."

"Michael Ryan," Elizabeth whispered. She shook her head. "Where will you go? What will become of you?"

"Well, with luck we'll find some place where we can conceal ourselves for the next six months or so. Dad's been miserable without my mom and my sister, so I know he'll try to find some way to get us all together again. Maybe somewhere in Europe will be safer."

Elizabeth bit her lip. "And you can't tell anyone? Not even me?"

He leaned over and stroked her hair. "You know the answer to that," he said sorrowfully. "Don't talk about it, Liz. It'll only be worse."

"I can't help it," she cried. "I can't believe that your dad is going to come downstairs with a suitcase and you two are just going to walk out of here forever!" She stared around her. "You can't just leave this place," she added hysterically. "What about the house? The furniture?"

"Liz, that isn't what matters." Michael looked at her intently. "You and I have learned about the stuff that counts. The real stuff. Like this." With that he leaned forward, his eyes intent on hers, and traced the outline of her lips with his finger. Elizabeth's eyes closed slowly, tears seeping out from beneath them as Michael lowered his face toward hers. She could just feel the warmth of his breath against her face when the door was kicked open and something clattered across the floor. The two jumped apart and stared with horror at the open door.

"Don't move." The man in the gray suit kicked the door open further. "Stay there, both of you." He inched forward into the room, two men following him—both with guns aimed directly at Elizabeth and Michael.

Elizabeth swallowed hard. She couldn't take her eyes away from the barrels of the guns pointing right at them. She recognized the man in the suit as the man who had followed her and Michael the first time they went out. And one of the other gunmen was the man who had stopped her and identified himself as an F.B.I. agent. Her stomach turned over in terror.

"Michael?" Mr. Hankman called unsuspectingly from upstairs. "Would you mind coming up here for a minute and giving me a hand with this suitcase?"

Elizabeth and Michael stared at each other, their eyes wide.

The man in the gray suit inched toward the staircase. For a minute Elizabeth was positive *he* was going to climb the stairs instead of Michael. But he spoke instead, his voice rough and mean.

"Throw it down, Ryan," he said. "And then please do us a favor and come down after it—with your hands high above your head. We've got some things to talk over."

Dr. Ryan didn't answer. After a long, tense moment the suitcase came bouncing down the stairs. Then Dr. Ryan followed, taking one step at a time. He looked at the three men with a mixture of hatred, anger, and resignation, but he didn't say a word.

"We happen to think you're mistaken about needing that little bag," the man continued with a nasty drawl. "Isn't that true, guys?" he asked the gunmen, who nodded, their eyes fixed on Dr. Ryan's face.

"As a matter of fact," the man continued, "we happen to think you and your son—and his pretty little girlfriend here—aren't going anywhere."

And with that awful declaration, he kicked the front door closed, trapping the Ryans and Elizabeth inside the house with him and the gunmen.

Fourteen

Dr. Ryan froze. It seemed to take him forever to recover his composure enough to kick the suitcase the rest of the way down and creep down the stairs with his hands up. Elizabeth could hear noises rooms away: the clock ticking in the kitchen, the purr of the air conditioner. Everything seemed sharply defined and more vivid, and at the same time unreal. The scene before her was so frightening it made her dizzy, and she had to grab onto a chair for support.

The two gunmen had assumed a crouching position in the space between the front door and the open archway to the living room. The man in the gray suit, clearly the spokesman, was pacing back and forth, his eyes flicking from Michael and Elizabeth to Dr. Ryan. After Dr. Ryan threw down the suitcase, nothing happened. They all stood still with the exception of the man in the suit, who paced. The clock ticked louder. Elizabeth realized she had been holding her breath, and when she let it out, bit by bit, she could see her knuckles were white from gripping the back of the chair so tightly.

"OK, Ryan," the man in gray said at last. "I think it's time for us to do a little talking. Only I think we'd better talk alone, don't you?"

Dr. Ryan turned and looked at Michael. His expression was so filled with love and devotion that Elizabeth felt her eyes fill with tears. "Michael," he said softly. "Will you go upstairs? Take Elizabeth into the small den and close the door. And don't move until this"—his voice broke briefly—"till this man tells you to."

Michael shivered, his face contorting with grief and anger. "I won't leave you, Dad," he said at last.

Then Elizabeth saw a new side of Dr. Ryan— the tough, courageous side that had allowed him to testify against DeLucca and to rescue the choking boy in the coffee shop. He drew himself up and glowered at Michael with a look that said *obey me*. Michael drew a long, quivering breath and crossed the living room in three steps to throw his arms around his father.

"Get upstairs," the man in the gray suit snapped. "Enough of this tearjerker nonsense. And take your girlfriend with you!"

Elizabeth felt a sob escape from her throat as Michael grabbed her hand and pulled her along with him to the staircase. She felt as if her feet had turned to lead. "Come on," Michael said, tugging at her arm. Suddenly the full horror of the situation hit her, and she raced up the stairs behind him.

In the den Michael sank down onto the couch, and Elizabeth sat down beside him, her head resting lightly on his shoulder. What could possibly happen now, she wondered. There seemed to be no way out of this awful mess.

She let out a long sigh, then gasped when she saw a small alarm box on the wall behind the coffee table. "Michael, look! Your father never disconnected the alarm system the last owner of this house installed! Push that red button, fast!"

"What is it?" Michael demanded, staring skeptically at the box.

Elizabeth reached around him and pressed the button as hard as she could.

"It's called the Good Neighbor system. When you push it, it goes off in six other houses in the area that are also part of the network—and in the police station. It's completely silent, so they won't know downstairs. Then one of the neighbors will call and say the first part of the password to your father. If he doesn't finish it, they'll come running right over to make sure he's all right."

Michael looked at Elizabeth in disbelief. "I can't believe any Good Neighbor system is going to be much help at this point.

Elizabeth pushed the red button again. "It can't hurt," she told him. "Michael, don't you have any faith in people at all?"

Michael shook his head. "Not when I think that one of those so-called good neighbors must have told those creeps downstairs where to find my dad and me. How else did they find out where we live?"

Elizabeth was aghast. "No one would have told them!" she cried. "Michael, you can't believe that!"

Michael shrugged. "Give me another explanation, then," he said.

Elizabeth shivered. She couldn't believe anyone would turn the Ryans in. "Why would anyone do that? Tell me one thing they'd have to gain," she demanded.

"Money," Michael said flatly. "What else? You know how much money my dad's life is worth now?" He shuddered. "Oh, Liz, I can't stand being up here knowing his life is in danger! I don't care what they said. I'm going downstairs."

"Michael, don't!" Elizabeth cried, grabbing his arm. Just then the telephone rang, and her fingers tightened. "It's working!" she cried. "Michael, the system's working!"

The man in the gray suit stared at the ringing phone, then at Dr. Ryan. "OK, Ryan, pick it up and act normal, you understand? One false word and you know what we'll do to you. Not to mention your son. You know we want to keep you alive till we find out what you both know. But we'll sacrifice you right now if we have to. Understand?"

Dr. Ryan nodded. On the third ring he picked up the phone. "Hello?" he said, trying to keep his voice calm.

"Hankman, are you all right?" It was Mr. Applebaum, who lived right next door. "If you are, say the password."

"I'm sorry," Dr. Ryan said, clearing his throat, "who did you ask for?" He kept his eye on the man in gray, who was looking at him suspiciously. "You must have the wrong number," he added.

"Just sit tight, Hankman. We're coming over," Mr. Applebaum cried.

Elizabeth and Michael had crept out of the den into the long corridor leading to the staircase. They listened to Dr. Ryan's conversation, then made their way slowly downstairs. They were almost at the bottom when they heard footsteps outside the front door. Just a few at first, then many. Before they knew what was happening, the door burst open, and the living room was swarming with people.

"Grab their guns!" Mr. Applebaum shouted. Frank Richman, the neighbor on the other side, tackled one of the gunmen and Mr. Simon from down the street tackled the other. Michael and Elizabeth ran to help Dr. Ryan, who was struggling with the man in gray behind the couch. The first gunman's weapon went clattering across the floor, and Frank Richman grabbed it. After a scuffle, Mr. Simon and another man managed to grab the second gunman and twist the gun out of his hand. Over twelve neighbors had hastened over to answer the alarm, and the gunmen were so badly outnumbered that they were forced to throw down their weapons—just as two squad cars, sirens wailing, pulled into the driveway and Jessica, Darcy, and Mr. Beckwith jumped out of the backseat of one of them.

"What's happened? Where's my sister?" Jessica cried, racing into the living room and searching around frantically for her twin.

"Jess!" Elizabeth cried. The next minute the two girls were hugging each other, laughing and crying at the same time. The Ryans' living room was a scene of total pandemonium. The policemen were handcuffing the man in gray and the two gunmen; Dr. Ryan was slapping Mr. Applebaum on the back; Michael was hugging Mr. Simon and then Frank Richman, and Mr. Beckwith and Darcy were gazing around in total confusion.

"What happened?" Darcy demanded.

"Well," Dr. Ryan said, taking off his glasses and wiping his eyes, "for one thing, I learned an important lesson from Miss Wakefield today." He gave Elizabeth a big smile. "I learned a little something about being a good citizen in Sweet Valley."

Michael put his arm around Elizabeth. "My dad isn't the only one who learned a lesson," he whispered. "You were right to trust people, Liz. I'll never forget what happened today. Not as long as I live."

The man in gray was glowering. "I wouldn't congratulate yourself too much, Ryan. They've got DeLucca now, and they've got me. But there are more of us. Many more. You and your family will never be safe. No matter where you hide, we'll keep tracking you down."

Dr. Ryan put his glasses back on. "I don't

know your name," he said coldly, "but I do know this: there are more of us than there are of you. And as long as there are good people in the world, people like these"—he made a broad sweeping gesture to include everyone in the room—"then my family *will* be safe. Maybe it won't be easy, but we're willing to fight."

"How did you find out where we were, anyway?" Michael demanded.

"Our people are everywhere too. You can't hide from us. Once we traced you to Sweet Valley, it was simple to locate your house. And by the way, we won't be needing this anymore." The man tossed him a blue notebook— badly tattered—which he removed from inside his jacket.

Jessica gasped. "Omigod, the notebook!"

"Don't worry," the man in the suit said gruffly. "It was of no use to us anyway."

Michael picked up the notebook and stared at it. He turned to Elizabeth. "But I thought *you* had it," he said, confused.

Elizabeth's eyebrows shot up. "Me? Why would I have it?"

"But you"—Michael shook his head—"you came over and asked me for it, remember?"

"Lizzie, don't be mad," Jessica pleaded. "I only did it because—" She stared helplessly at Darcy. "You tell her, Darcy."

"We thought we had to protect you from Eric," Darcy explained, looking miserable. "My friend Sue kept giving me all this information that made me think Eric"—she hesitated— "that Eric was really Christopher Wyeth, this guy who's wanted for murder in Ohio. So Jessica and I have been trying to figure out whether or not Eric was really the killer."

"You've lost me," Dr. Ryan said, shaking his head.

The older of the two policemen had overheard part of this conversation. "Chris Wyeth? The guy who murdered those girls in Ohio? He was caught last night!" he exclaimed.

Darcy stared sheepishly at the floor. "I guess Sue isn't a very reliable source of information. But Eric *looked* like him a little bit," she added helplessly.

"What about the notebook?" Michael demanded.

"Well, I made Jessica pretend to be Liz and ask you for it. We thought we could find out more about you if we read it."

"Only I never even got to look at it," Jessica said regretfully, "because he"—she pointed at the man in gray—"knocked me off my bike and stole it."

Elizabeth moaned. "Boy, I really wish someone had considered *telling* me some of these things."

"Well, the important thing is that we're all OK," Michael said. He stared at Darcy. "You thought I was a *mur*derer?"

Darcy turned beet red. "Well—I—uh—I didn't at first! I thought you were really neat. It's just—"

Michael shook his head. "Never mind," he muttered. "I have a feeling there's a lot going on here I'd prefer to leave a mystery."

"But you see," Elizabeth said warmly, "no one turned you in. I knew they wouldn't!"

Michael threw his arms around her and gave her a big hug.

"OK, everyone, clear the way. We're taking these three down to the station," the policeman said.

Dr. Ryan watched the police lead off the gunmen. When the front door had closed behind them, he put up his hand.

"Listen," he said in a loud, clear voice. "I want to thank all of you for what you did. You saved my life—and probably the life of my son and Elizabeth Wakefield, too. You're all very brave." He sighed. "It's going to be hard to leave you. But Michael and I do have to go—as soon as possible, even before the night is over. I just didn't want any one of you to leave this house without knowing how deeply moved I am by what you've all done. Apart from saving our lives, you reminded me what it is to be part of a real community." He dabbed the tears from her eyes. "One of the hardest things about the life we're forced to lead now is that we can't really belong to any community for long. We're going to have to keep moving, keep changing our appearance and our names. But you've reminded me tonight that we're all members of one big community, whatever we look like and whatever we call ourselves. We're all human beings. And as long as we believe in right and wrong, we're all fighting the same fight."

This speech was greeted with tremendous applause. Michael's eyes were shining with tears. "He's a wonderful man, my father," he murmured.

"And he has a wonderful son," Elizabeth said softly, fighting hard to hold back her tears.

Dr. Ryan said they had to leave that very night. How in the world was she going to face saying goodbye to Michael?

Fifteen

By nine o'clock the Ryans' house was almost back to normal. The police and the neighbors were long gone. Jessica and Darcy had hurried back to Darcy's house to call Sue in Ohio to tell her that Eric Hankman wasn't a murderer at all.

Finally only Elizabeth was left.

"Michael," Dr. Ryan said, putting his hand on his son's shoulder, "the police are giving us full protection tonight so we can get to the airport. Our flight leaves in two hours." He looked awkwardly at Elizabeth. "I'm afraid it doesn't give you two very much time to say goodbye."

Elizabeth swallowed hard. "What matters most is that you get out of here safely," she said. She was trying hard to be brave. It was impossible for her to imagine that once Michael left she would never be able to talk to him on the phone or even write him a letter. He would drop out of her life forever.

When Dr. Ryan left the room, she started to tell Michael how she felt. "How am I going to stand not knowing if you're all right?"

Michael hugged her tightly. "You'll know. And one day maybe all of this rotten stuff will be over, and we'll be able to come out of hiding. You know the first thing I'll do is come back to you."

Elizabeth couldn't hold the tears back any longer. "Oh, Michael," she cried, burying her face in his neck.

Michael pulled away slightly so he could look at her face. "I'm never going to forget you, Elizabeth," he said solemnly. "My dad was right when he said all those things tonight. You've taught us both something about courage."

"Me?" Elizabeth said. "But you're the ones who have courage."

"I mean the courage to trust people," Michael said gently. He put his finger to her lips to keep her from speaking. "Like the way I trust you," he added.

Elizabeth didn't think she could bear it any longer. "I'm not sure I'm going to be able to stand it, watching you two leave," she said, her voice breaking.

"Well, then, you'll have to be the first to leave," Michael said tenderly. "I'll walk you to your car."

Elizabeth followed him to the front door. Before they left the house, Michael bent down and picked up the blue notebook the man in gray had tossed on the coffee table. It was his notebook of poems. "I should have known you would never have asked me for this," he mused. He gave Elizabeth a long, searching look. "Will you keep this for me?" he asked her. "It's yours anyway. Everything in it is for you."

Elizabeth gasped. "Not your poems! Oh, Michael, I couldn't!"

"I want you to have them, Liz. When you get into bed tonight, read the poem on the last page. I wrote it for you this weekend when I thought something might come between us. It describes what I feel for you."

Elizabeth nodded. "I'll keep the notebook. But you have to let me give you something in exchange."

"Oh, Liz," Michael said, folding her in his arms for a last embrace. "You've given me the most wonderful gift in the world. You've made me believe in people again."

Elizabeth couldn't find a way to answer him. But she knew the look in her eyes told him everything she was feeling, and more.

"I can't believe you!" Jessica cried. She and Darcy were in the Wakefields' living room waiting for Elizabeth to get home. "Don't you even feel the tiniest bit embarrassed about thinking Eric—or Michael, or whoever he is—was a murderer?"

"It wasn't my fault," Darcy said indignantly. "I was only trying to protect Liz."

"Yeah," Jessica said morosely. "But you made us both look like giant jerks in the meantime. The more I think about it, the more absurd the whole thing seems. I mean, Eric just doesn't seem like a murderer, Darcy. I ought to have known better." She regarded Darcy imperiously. "After all, I was a *witness* to a murder—or at least to the planting of a body. I got chased by a murderer. I know what murderers look like. And they definitely don't look like Eric Hankman!"

"That's just great," Darcy said huffily. "Don't you think you could have pointed that out a little bit earlier? You were as suspicious as I was, Jess."

Jessica frowned. She was beginning to think

she might have been wrong about Darcy Kaymen. Instead of apologizing profusely for having put her through all this trouble and embarrassment, Darcy just acted as if it had all been a simple mistake. Jessica thought the least she could do was to try to make it up, maybe by offering to do Jessica's work at the office or something.

But Darcy seemed completely unashamed. In fact, she didn't even wait for Elizabeth to get home. She said she was tired, and she left, just as Jessica's parents came in with Adam and Steven.

"Weren't you worried about us?" Jessica demanded when they entered the living room. "Lizzie and I were in terrible danger." Her eyes were big as she proceeded to describe what had happened. "Guess whose house we were at tonight? Dr. Ryan's, the man who testified against Frank DeLucca!"

"Yeah, and then you went to Mars," Steven scoffed, leaning over to rumple her hair.

"Jessica, what on earth are you talking about?" Mrs. Wakefield demanded.

"Mr. Hankman," Jessica explained calmly, "turns out to be Dr. Ryan and not Mr. Hankman at all. His son isn't who we thought he was either," she muttered, half to herself.

Just then the front door opened, and Elizabeth came into the foyer. Her face was streaked with tears, and she was clutching a blue note-book to her chest.

"Why, sweetheart, whatever—" Mrs. Wake-field hurried over to put her arms around her, but Elizabeth pulled away, shaking.

"I need to be alone right now," she said brokenly. And before anyone could say any-thing, she hurried upstairs, slamming the odor to her bedroom.

At first Elizabeth couldn't bear to look at the notebook Michael had given her. She tried to sleep, but her dreams were interrupted by mem-ories so poignant and vivid that her tears would begin anew. Finally, she couldn't stand it any-more, and she turned on the light and picked up the notebook from the table beside her bed. Just looking at Michael's small handwriting made her ache all over with sadness. She wondered where the Ryans were now. Where were they flying? Would they be safe?

She swallowed hard, trying to be brave. She had promised Michael that she would continue to believe the best—about people, about fate—and that she would believe he and his family were safe, and together, whenever she thought of him. But it was going to be very hard.

She turned to the last page of the notebook,

her fingers trembling. The poem, written in Michael's neat handwriting, was called "Goodbye Poem." The first time she read it her eyes blurred so badly with tears she could hardly make out the words. But the second time it all came through to her with incredible clarity and sadness. It was as if Michael were right there saying the words to her:

Goodbye Poem

To say we touched
To say you taught me
To say I saw things new
To say I love you—
none of these is enough,
my friend.

For your world
with all its light and hope
couldn't prepare me for this
sorrow, this saying
goodbye.

Tell me it won't matter.
Promise me wherever I am
you will be with me
in the place where "goodbye"
doesn't matter, where "forever"

> is just an instant, and our love
> a bridge, connecting,
> linking, making all things one.

Elizabeth put the notebook down, the tears streaming down her face. She didn't know if she would ever find that place Michael had described. But she knew she would never forget him, not as long as she lived.

"It's hard to believe that it was only Monday when all that stuff happened," Darcy said. It was Wednesday morning, and she was sitting at her desk in the *News* office, looking absent-mindedly at a story about Chris Wyeth, who was in jail in Ohio without bail.

"Yeah." Jessica glanced at Elizabeth to see what her reaction would be. "It seems like ages ago already."

Elizabeth didn't answer. The memories were so clear in her mind she could hardly believe any time had elapsed since Michael and his father had left.

"I wonder where the Ryans are now," Darcy said, completely unaware that this might not be the best topic to bring up in front of Elizabeth.

But Elizabeth seemed stoic. "I hope they're far away from people like that awful man in the gray suit," she said with a shudder. "I just hope they're safe."

Now that Darcy had gotten started she seemed ready for a good long talk about Elizabeth's personal life. "What are you going to do about Jeffrey, Liz?" she asked with interest. "You're not going to tell him about what happened with Eric—I mean, Michael—are you?"

Elizabeth stared at her. "That's kind of a personal question, don't you think?" she asked calmly.

Jessica was listening with fascination. She herself had been more than a little curious about this very question, but she had been afraid to bring it up until Elizabeth seemed a little less sensitive about it.

"I just wondered," Darcy said briskly. "You don't have to get upset, Liz."

Elizabeth didn't say anything. She knew eventually she and Jeffrey would have to have a long talk. And she would have to try to figure out what difference her feelings for Michael had made in her life. But she couldn't think about that now. It was all too recent, and the pain of parting too fresh.

For now she just had to remember what the Ryans had taught her about courage. And that meant believing that they would be safe and that Michael was thinking about her with the same incredible fondness that she was thinking about him.

"You know," Jessica said thoughtfully, "it's kind of strange how many weird things have happened around here this summer. Think about it. First we saw Tom Winslow with Laurie's body, and there was that terrible couple of weeks when the police thought Adam had killed her. And then Mr. Hankman and his son show up, and they turn out to be government heroes in disguise, chased by figures from the underworld." She sat back in her chair and stared up at the ceiling. "Kind of makes you wonder what's going to happen next, doesn't it?"

Darcy gave her a condescending look. "I already *know* what's going to happen next. We're going to get a bunch of new tedious assignments from Dan and Seth."

Jessica ignored this comment. She happened to think Darcy was wrong. As far as she could tell, Sweet Valley was starting to be a pretty exciting place to be. She wondered what kind of mystery was going to turn up next.

SWEET VALLEY HIGH

☐	27650	**AGAINST THE ODDS #51**	$2.95
☐	27720	**WHITE LIES #52**	$2.95
☐	27771	**SECOND CHANCE #53**	$2.95
☐	27856	**TWO BOY WEEKEND #54**	$2.95
☐	27915	**PERFECT SHOT #55**	$2.95
☐	27970	**LOST AT SEA #56**	$2.95
☐	28079	**TEACHER CRUSH #57**	$2.95
☐	28156	**BROKEN HEARTS #58**	$2.95
☐	28193	**IN LOVE AGAIN #59**	$2.95
☐	28264	**THAT FATAL NIGHT #60**	$2.95

Buy them at your local bookstore or use this page to order.

Bantam Books, Dept. SVH7, 414 East Golf Road, Des Plaines, IL 60016

Please send me the items I have checked above. I am enclosing $_____
(please add $2.00 to cover postage and handling). Send check or money
order, no cash or C.O.D.s please.

Mr/Ms _____

Address _____

City/State _____ Zip_____

SVH7–11/89

Please allow four to six weeks for delivery.
Prices and availability subject to change without notice.

☐	27590	**BITTER RIVALS #29**	$2.95
☐	27558	**JEALOUS LIES #30**	$2.95
☐	27490	**TAKING SIDES #31**	$2.95
☐	27560	**THE NEW JESSICA #32**	$2.95
☐	27491	**STARTING OVER #33**	$2.95
☐	27521	**FORBIDDEN LOVE #34**	$2.95
☐	27666	**OUT OF CONTROL #35**	$2.95
☐	27662	**LAST CHANCE #36**	$2.95
☐	27884	**RUMORS #37**	$2.95
☐	27631	**LEAVING HOME #38**	$2.95
☐	27691	**SECRET ADMIRER #39**	$2.95
☐	27692	**ON THE EDGE #40**	$2.95
☐	27693	**OUTCAST #41**	$2.95
☐	26951	**CAUGHT IN THE MIDDLE #42**	$2.95
☐	27006	**HARD CHOICES #43**	$2.95
☐	27064	**PRETENSES #44**	$2.95
☐	27176	**FAMILY SECRETS #45**	$2.95
☐	27278	**DECISIONS #46**	$2.95
☐	27359	**TROUBLEMAKER #47**	$2.95
☐	27416	**SLAM BOOK FEVER #48**	$2.95
☐	27477	**PLAYING FOR KEEPS #49**	$2.95
☐	27596	**OUT OF REACH #50**	$2.95

Buy them at your local bookstore or use this page to order.

Bantam Books, Dept. SVH2, 414 East Golf Road, Des Plaines, IL 60016

Please send me the items I have checked above. I am enclosing $_____
(please add $2.00 to cover postage and handling). Send check or money
order, no cash or C.O.D.s please.

Mr/Ms _____

Address _____

City/State_____ Zip_____

Please allow four to six weeks for delivery.
Prices and availability subject to change without notice.

SVH2–11/89

Special Offer
Buy a Bantam Book
for only 50¢.

Now you can order the exciting books you've been wanting to read straight from Bantam's latest catalog of hundreds of titles. And this special offer gives you the opportunity to purchase a Bantam book for only 50¢. Here's how:

By ordering any five books at the regular price per order, you can also choose any other single book listed (up to a $5.95 value) for only 50¢. Some restrictions do apply, so for further details send for Bantam's catalog of titles today!

Just send us your name and address and we will send you Bantam Book's SHOP AT HOME CATALOG!